The faded sign was the same one that had been there for as long as Neal could remember. He was hands-down the most unwelcome person ever to enter Rivermist. But somewhere between his apartment and the office that morning, he'd accepted the inevitable. He had to make sure his father was all right.

He'd been so certain staying away the past three years was the right thing. He'd finally faced his mistakes and he'd moved on. But second thoughts had hounded him the entire drive over.

Neal shoved the transmission into Reverse. Gripping the steering wheel, he fantasized about turning around and barreling back to Atlanta and the people he could actually help. Then with a curse he yanked the gearshift back to Neutral and set the hand brake.

"Jennifer Gardner."

There. He'd said her name, and it hadn't hurt a bit. With the discipline that came from years of practice, he refused to let her face materialize in his mind. But as always, the perfection of her crystal-clear laugh haunted him.

What if she was still in Rivermist?

Dear Reader,

You can never go home again, or so the saying goes. You can look back and yearn for a simpler time, or wish that things might have been different, but rewriting the past is beyond man's power.

But since yesterday plays a hand in our future, in who we are now, gazing back is about so much more than longing and reminiscing. We see ourselves most clearly sometimes in our mistakes and failures, and in the journey we take as we make our way back home.

In *The Prodigal's Return* our hero and heroine face what they've fought for years to outrun and learn to find strength in how far they've come. To claim the freedom of accepting what is broken and in letting that weakness guide them to their second chance.

The weakest thing inside us often holds the promise of our greatest strength. And the lowest man in our midst can be the key to others soaring to their greatest heights—if only they can see that unconditional love is the source of forgiveness, and that it is in the heart that second chances are born.

Whether your dream is to return to a life left unfinished, or to reclaim a loved one let go too soon, I wish for you the acceptance and understanding and hope you'll need along your journey. Trust your heart to lead the way, and what you are seeking will come back to you.

Blessings,

Anna DeStefano

PS. I love to hear from readers. Come join me at my Web site and in my daily journal at www.annawrites.com.

THE PRODIGAL'S RETURN

Anna DeStefano

HARLEQUIN®

TORONTO • NEW YORK • LONDON
AMSTERDAM • PARIS • SYDNEY • HAMBURG
STOCKHOLM • ATHENS • TOKYO • MILAN • MADRID
PRAGUE • WARSAW • BUDAPEST • AUCKLAND

ISBN-13: 978-0-373-71358-5
ISBN-10:   0-373-71358-4

THE PRODIGAL'S RETURN

Books by Anna DeStefano

HARLEQUIN SUPERROMANCE

Don't miss any of our special offers. Write to us at the
following address for information on our newest releases.

Harlequin Reader Service
U.S.: 3010 Walden Ave., P.O. Box 1325, Buffalo, NY 14269
Canadian: P.O. Box 609, Fort Erie, Ont. L2A 5X3

For my editor, Johanna Raisanen.
Your touch flourishes in so much that I do,
but *The Prodigal's Return* more than others is yours.

This story was years in the making,
but I can't imagine not having taken the journey,
or not having you there at each turn.
I pray others, as they read, see what I see:
your glorious patience and wisdom shining from every word.

For my agent, Michelle Grajkowski.
You are generosity and strength and grace personified.
You believed in the heart of this story
long before anyone else, even I, did.
It's your confidence and encouragement
that helped me find my own faith.

PROLOGUE

"DO YOU SWEAR to tell the truth, the whole truth, and nothing but the truth, so help you God?" a courtroom officer asked sixteen-year-old Jennifer Gardner.

"What?" She blinked at the bailiff who stood before the witness box, tearing her gaze away from where Neal Cain slouched beside his father at the defendant's table.

Tell the truth.

That's what Neal wanted her to do, or so his dad had said.

He knows the prosecutor's going to call you to testify, Mr. Cain had insisted as he'd prepped her that morning. He'd been more a surrogate father at that moment than the county's top defense attorney. *Don't be afraid. Just answer the D.A.'s questions, and everything will be fine.*

But normally fun-loving Mr. Cain had looked worried. After his wife's death ten years ago, he'd built his world around his son and his law practice. Now, Neal was on trial for involuntary manslaughter.

Mr. Cain didn't believe everything was going to be *fine* any more than Jenn did.

"Miss Gardner?" Judge Pritchard's voice dragged her attention to where he sat on a dais beside her. "Even though this is merely an arraignment to determine if a trial is warranted, you are required to speak the full and complete truth, under risk of perjury. Do you understand?"

She nodded, and the legal proceeding began, with every eye in the room locked on her—all of them but Neal's. She fought not to throw up as the district attorney took the bailiff's place and forced her to relive the worst night of her life, one painful memory at a time. Like a vulture, he kept circling the fact that she'd allegedly chosen to leave the homecoming dance early, to walk the mile and a half home, alone, in her formal gown.

"Did you by any chance arrange to meet Bobby Compton at his car?" The ugly suspicion in D.A. Burnside's question echoed what many in town had been thinking for weeks.

"No!" Jenn said to the entire courtroom. "I was going home. That's all."

Good little Jennifer Gardner, her father's secretary had whispered to Mary Jo Reece last Sunday. She hadn't noticed Jenn and her mother sitting only a pew away, so why bother with the charity and tolerance Jenn's pastor father expected from his staff.

I just can't believe it. The preacher's daughter, making out in the school parking lot. Drinking. Lord knows what else. And those two boys fighting over her. She was leading them both on, everyone thinks so. What else could it have been…?

"I didn't know I'd run into Bobby when I left," Jenn said, her tears blurring the D.A.'s face.

"Your statement to the sheriff says you became angry with Bobby Compton at the dance." Mr. Burnside made a show of reading notes from a file.

"Yes, because—"

"Yet you left early without your date, so you could have a private moment with the boy in a deserted parking lot? A boy the defendant had just been fighting with."

"Yes—no! I left early, but not to talk with Bobby. It wasn't like that."

The D.A.'s forehead wrinkled in confusion. "You told the sheriff you got into Bobby Compton's car."

"I couldn't let him drive home the way he was." She glanced at her dad.

Concern filled Joshua Gardner's eyes. Sadness. Disappointment that she'd never seen, before a few weeks ago. Never thought was possible. Not from the man who'd been her hero. Her rock.

"Drunk, you mean?" the lawyer asked.

"What?"

"You stopped because you thought Bobby was drunk?"

"Yes. I…I'd seen him drinking at the dance."

"And were you and Neal drunk as well?"

"No!"

Her parents and their pricey Atlanta lawyer had insisted that she not speak with anyone about that night, not even to defend herself against the rumors flying all over town.

"But you *had* been drinking with the deceased?"

"Y-yes." Her father closed his eyes, crossed his arms, as the courtroom's attention shifted his way. It had sent shock waves through the county, the preacher's child admitting to the police that she'd been drinking since she was thirteen. "Bobby, Neal and some of the other football players snuck some beer in. A lot of us were drinking it, but Neal and I weren't dru—"

"But Neal and Bobby *had* been fighting before you decided to leave the dance?"

"Y-yes."

"Because Mr. Compton kissed you on the dance floor?"

"Bobby… He'd just broken up with Stephie Blake. He was upset. I was talking with him, trying to make him feel better… To get him to stop drinking. He said I was being so sweet, that Neal was lucky… Then…I'm not really sure how it happened, but—"

"Bobby Compton kissed you?"

She chewed her lip, shuddering at the memory of the argument that had followed. Bobby trying to shrug off Neal's hand, hauling her even closer. Neal's accusing glare as it shifted between her and his best friend. Her plea to Bobby to stop it. To let her go.

"Miss Gardner?" the D.A. pressed.

"Yes." Neal wouldn't look at her, no matter how long she stared. He hadn't spoken to her since the night Bobby died. "He kissed me."

Shock whispered through the room.

"And he and the defendant fought?"

"They… Neal was angry, and Bobby wasn't thinking straight."

"How long have you and the defendant been dating?"

"Almost two years." The most perfect years of her life.

"Yet, you kissed his best friend right in front of him?"

"Bobby kissed me—"

"Would it surprise you to learn, that I have eye-witnesses from that night who would testify to the contrary? Maybe you wanted your boyfriend to see you kissing—"

"Objection, Your Honor." Mr. Cain shot to his feet. "Miss Gardner's behavior is not on trial. It's irrelevant to these proceedings who kissed whom, or why."

It took several pounds of the judge's gavel to settle the room.

"Mr. Burnside," he warned. "Keep your questions focused on the defendant's actions."

"So," the prosecutor continued with a nod, "the defendant and Bobby Compton fought over you at the homecoming dance. Mr. Compton left. Then you followed him."

"I didn't follow Bobby."

The D.A. laid his folder on the witness box's ledge. It was open to a report that ended with Neal's signature. "The statement the defendant gave the sheriff says that when he found you, you were inside the car with Bobby."

"Yes. I took Bobby's keys away so he couldn't drive home. He asked me to sit with him while he cleared his head."

"You sat together?"

"Yes."

"In his car?"

"Yes."

"And then?"

Jenn swallowed the lump her breakfast kept making in her throat. "Bobby grabbed me again."

"Your Honor!" Mr. Cain was on his feet once more. Neal stayed seated, his fists clenched on the tabletop.

"I tried to stop him," she insisted.

"Get to your point, Mr. Burnside," Judge Pritchard warned.

The D.A. placed his hands on his hips, every speck of friendliness gone from his unsmiling face.

"Miss Gardner, please describe for the court Neal Cain's reaction when he found you *trying to stop* the advances of his best friend."

"Neal was angry. He was hurt."

A hollow weight settled on her chest. If Neal would only let her close again, maybe then she could survive everyone else deserting her, even her parents. She searched his downcast features, desperate for any sign that he hadn't given up—on both himself and on her.

D.A. Burnside retrieved the folder from in front of her. "The defendant pulled Bobby Compton from the car?"

"Yes." Her stomach took another threatening roll upward.

"And they began to fight again."

"Yes."

"And the defendant hit the victim."

"They were hitting each other." She brushed at her tears. If only there were some way to wipe away the memories. "I tried to stop them—"

"You tried to stop the defendant?"

"Yes… No! Both of them. I tried to stop them both."

"But you couldn't."

"No. And then Bobby fell and he… He hit his head against the curb."

After a long pause, the D.A. plucked more papers from his briefcase. "The police report states that while Bobby Compton received a blow to the head— one we now know was the contributing cause of his death—the defendant escaped the confrontation with little more than a black eye. If they were fighting each other, as you say, how do you account for the defendant's lack of injuries?"

"I don't know." She gripped the edge of her straight-back chair. "Maybe because Bobby was drunk, and Neal was—"

"Angry?" the D.A. offered.

"Neal didn't mean to hurt him." She turned to address the judge directly. "They were best friends."

"But Bobby Compton *was* hurt," the D.A. interjected. "He was taken to the hospital in an ambulance, where he later died. While Neal Cain spent that night, and every night since, sleeping peacefully in his own bed."

"But he hasn't. I don't think he's slept at all." And anyone who thought differently didn't know him. Neal had already convicted himself for Bobby's death—so had the rest of the town. But she couldn't.

She never would. "He's devastated by what happened. He's lost his best friend."

"And Bobby Compton lost his life," D.A. Burnside added softly, his words carrying through the now-silent room.

A stifled sob drew everyone's attention to the back, to the very last row of benches. Mrs. Compton, her face partially buried against her husband's burly chest, was shaking, clinging to him.

Jenn closed her eyes against the sight of the same shock and grief that were eating her and Neal alive. She looked to her father for... For what?

Understanding? Forgiveness?

Not a chance.

Not for her.

Not now.

It was as if her parents had become strangers to her.

"Please, stop this," a heart-breakingly familiar voice begged.

Her head jerked around to find Neal on his feet beside his father, pulling away from Mr. Cain's grasp.

"Sit down!" Mr. Cain bit out.

"Stop it, Dad." Neal faced the judge. "Your Honor, for the sake of Bobby Compton's family, please, call this off."

"Neal!" Mr. Cain looked ready to deck his son to

keep him quiet, but Jenn knew he loved Neal too much to ever hurt him.

She'd always marveled at the bond, the honesty, between them. At how much they even looked alike, despite the difference in their ages. They shared the same blond good looks, the same height and effortless athleticism and dreamy dark eyes. The same intensity when they were determined to have their way, as both were now.

"Your Honor," Mr. Cain pleaded. "My son's distraught over his friend's death. He doesn't understand—"

"I *do* understand." Neal's voice was the scariest calm Jenn had ever heard. "And I want to plead guilty."

"No!" Jenn and Mr. Cain cried in unison.

The room burst into a sea of babbling voices.

"That's enough." Judge Pritchard's gavel rapped. He leveled an accusing stare at the spectators. "I'll have no more outbursts, or this courtroom will be cleared."

When silence returned, it was harder to bear than the gossipy confusion it replaced. Because in the room's quiet, nothing remained but the end that Jenn knew she'd never survive.

Judge Pritchard returned his attention to the defendant's table.

"Have a seat, Mr. Cain."

"But, Your Honor—"

"Have a seat!"

"Son," the judge said when Neal was standing alone. "Do you understand the consequences of what you're saying? You're not being charged as a juvenile. You'll serve your sentence in an adult correctional facility."

"Yes, sir. My father's explained everything to me. I'm pleading guilty to involuntary manslaughter, and I'm going to prison. It's where I belong. We all know that. Don't put Bobby's parents through the motions of a trial that won't change anything."

"Neal." Mr. Cain's voice sounded too old, too lost, to belong to the fearless defense attorney prosecutors all over the state dreaded facing in a courtroom. "Please, we can find another way."

Please.

Jenn wanted to run to Neal. To beg along with his dad. But she couldn't move. Worse, nothing she said would make the tiniest difference.

"I told you this morning, Dad." Neal shook off his father's touch one last time. "I have to do this."

His gaze finally connected with Jenn's, his dark eyes at first apologizing, then emptying of every promise and dream they'd shared.

"Bobby's gone because of me." He continued to stare, through each awful word, as if to be sure she understood most of all. "There is no other way. It's over."

CHAPTER ONE

Midtown Atlanta, Georgia
Eight years later

"YOUR DADDY WOULDN'T call you himself, Neal, but somethin's not right." Buford Richmond's slow Southern drawl blended into the phone's staticky connection like a bad omen. "I'd bet money the man's sick."

Since Buford had laid down good money on the Birmingham races every Saturday for the past twenty years, the man *not* betting might have been more cause for concern. Still, Neal gave up pretending to work.

Your daddy wouldn't call you himself....

That was the God's honest truth.

There'd been no contact between him and his father for ages. Not since their last fight a year into his eight-year sentence. He'd refused, again, to file for early parole, still naively determined to do right by Bobby. As if pissing away his own life would bring his friend back, or give the boy's family a speck of peace. Exactly his father's point. But Neal hadn't been ready to hear reason then, and his father had shouted that he wouldn't be returning.

Not for the next month's visitation. Not ever. If Neal wanted to give up, if he thought rotting in prison would somehow make up for Bobby's death, that didn't mean his father had to watch.

You're a selfish sonovabitch, Nathan had railed. Thinking of the man as *Dad* hadn't been possible after that day. *You don't know how to do anything but quit. And you don't care who you're hurting by giving up. Well, I've hurt enough. I can't do this anymore.*

And neither could Neal.

Nathan giving up had been the right thing for both of them. A fitting end, leaving all ties neatly severed.

So why had Neal's heart slammed into his throat at the suggestion that the man might be sick?

He shoved aside the papers on his desk. *Focus on the here and now*—that's what he'd promised himself after that final argument. *Let go of Nathan. Let go of Bobby. Let go of the past.*

Survive.

Never look back.

That's what had gotten him through the remainder of his sentence. Nothing much had changed three years after his early release—parole garnered by model behavior, instead of his father's legendary briefs. Briefs Neal studied religiously now, to learn everything he could.

He wasn't a lawyer like his father. He never would be. But kicking legal ass consumed his time all the same, the way studying law books had those endless days and nights in his cell. Giving back, making up, it was a decent enough life. It made forgetting possible. At least it had until Buford's call.

His father's ex-law partner, Neal's only remaining contact to Rivermist, touched base from time to time to discuss financial matters. Rarely by phone. A registered letter from prison was all it had taken to give Buford temporary power of attorney over Neal's mother's sizable trust, set up for Neal after her death when he'd been only five. Ever since, they'd had an understanding. If Neal wanted to talk about his father, he'd ask. And he never had.

"My father's a very wealthy man." Neal rocked back in his secondhand desk chair, in the shabby office that was more a home than the tiny apartment he rented. Rubbed at the tension throbbing at the base of his neck. It was late in the afternoon. He'd cast off his suit coat and rolled up the starched sleeves of his dress shirt hours ago. And a long, solitary night of work stretched ahead—exactly the way he liked it. "If Nathan's sick, he'll find himself a doctor and get it taken care of."

"How much do you know about your daddy's situation?"

"I know he's alive. That he wants me out of his way. He has the means to take care of himself. There's no reason for me to be involved."

"I'm not sure Nathan wants to take care of himself—hang all that money he has in the bank." Buford, a litigator skilled at finessing juries into believing whatever version of the truth he represented, sounded a bit like a man feeling his way barefoot through shattered glass. "I wouldn't have called you if I thought he was doing okay, or that he'd listen to anyone else."

"Have you even talked with him since he dissolved your law partnership?"

"I tried." Buford chuckled. "The bastard actually challenged me to a fistfight the one time I stopped by the house."

One of Buford's first letters to Neal had explained the breakup of his and Nathan's friendship, as well as their law practice. He'd asked if it made a difference in Neal's feelings about Buford handling his money. Since Neal had stopped feeling anything by then, he'd assured Buford it hadn't mattered a bit.

The more distance, the better.

"So why involve yourself in his life now?" he demanded, needing every bit of that distance back.

"Nathan's and my history isn't the point, son. When your daddy lost you, he did some terrible things out of grief. I forgave him for that years ago. That man introduced me to my wife. He's godfather to my two girls. There's nothing I wouldn't do for him, even if he is too stubborn to ask for help. He's lived alone all this time, and I was happy to leave him be. But that don't mean I think he's been taking very good care of himself. And now—"

"Buford, I…" Damn it, looking the other way hadn't hurt this much in years. Nothing had. "I can't get involved."

His chance to make amends with Nathan…with anyone else…was long gone. Cutting the people who loved him out of his life had been a conscious choice. The horror of prison would have been unbearable if he hadn't moved on. And afterward, inflicting himself on the people he'd left behind, would have been cruel.

Some mistakes shouldn't be fixed. Opening a door to the past now, just a crack, meant unraveling everything. Every rotting memory he'd buried, worming its way back to the surface.

And for what?

"I know you're busy." Buford's tone inched perilously close to wheedling. "And the work you're doing there is important. But, if you could just see how bad the man looks, what little Nathan comes to town anymore—"

"I can't." An image of his father's devastated expression as he'd walked away that last time escaped the pit Neal had banished it to. Fast on its heels came the echo of Jennifer Gardner's sobbing on the witness stand, the heartbreaking picture she'd made as she'd listened to him finish destroying what they might have had together.

Jennifer.

He no longer felt anything for her most of all.

"There's nothing I can say to change your mind?" the lawyer asked.

"You knew the answer to that before you called." Neal squeezed his eyes shut.

"Yeah. Guess I did." The pause that followed conjured up a picture of Buford kicking back in his own beaten-up chair. "Don't hold it against an old man for trying. Can't help it if I think it would do both you and your daddy some good if you made your peace before it's too late."

Before it's too late…

Warning bells stopped tickling and began clamoring at the back of Neal's mind. He was being played by a crafty attorney, but it didn't seem to matter.

"I'd better let you get back to it." The master manipulator sighed. "I hear you're busting judicial balls in Atlanta. If your daddy only knew what you've been up to with your mama's money, he'd bust a gut—"

"Buford," Neal said through clenched teeth, biting down hard on a curse. He never cursed. He never lost his cool. To the world he now ruled, he was buttoned-down, spiffed-up professionalism at its best—with just enough of the hardness he hid deep edging through, to keep people conveniently off balance at work, and happy to leave him to his privacy everywhere else.

"Yeah?" The lawyer's faceless reply was hope at its *gotcha* best.

Neal stared at the folders sprawled across his desk. Paperwork representing the lives of people he barely knew who'd turned to him for help because they'd exhausted all other possibilities. He was their last hope. Atlanta's prince of saving lost causes. All of them but his own.

Damn it!

"Give me the name of my father's doctor," he heard himself say.

"Doc Harden's the only one your daddy would ever go to." Neal could hear the sly smile that warmed each Southern-tinged word. "But even if Doc knows something, I'm not sure he'd talk it over with you. He certainly wouldn't with me, the closed-mouth son of a gun. Whatever's going on, someone's pretty much going to have to bust your daddy's door down to get to the bottom of it."

"I'll make a few calls, that's it," Neal said. The phone slamming into its cradle cut off Buford's next sentence.

Just a few calls, that was all. One to the doctor,

one to his father. Simple enough, and he'd be done. Except contacting his old man would result in the kind of backlash no one wanted, him least of all.

He'd had his reasons for shutting down. Shutting the world out. Damn good ones. And his old man had bailed, too. If Nathan was lonely now, it was by choice, same as Neal. And alone suited Neal just fine.

The arguments were solid. Logical. Best for everyone.

So why did he suddenly feel like a class-A bastard for allowing the silence between him and his old man to drag on for seven years?

Whatever it takes, that had been his mantra in prison. He'd been a vulnerable kid who hadn't a clue what he'd set himself up for. A pretty boy, and everything his father had feared would happen had come at him like a demented welcome party as soon as he'd been placed in general population. He'd learned fast to do and say and fight however he'd had to, until the filthy predators with filthy hands, and the memories screaming how much he had lost, finally let him be.

In a matter of months, the pretty boy had died and the man he was never meant to be had taken the kid's place.

A man rumored to have no emotions, no fear. Only here he was, turning chicken-shit at the thought of making a couple of phone calls to check on the father he supposedly hadn't cared about for years.

Rivermist, Georgia

JENN GARDNER nearly ran over the old man before she saw him wandering down the middle of the road. Screeching to a halt mere inches away, she tracked his unsteady, weaving journey across North Street.

"Critter," he yelled into the evening's darkness. "Where the heck did you get off to this time? Crrritterrrr…"

She glanced at the clock on her ancient Civic's dashboard. She'd only been back in Rivermist for three months, and she hadn't yet gotten acclimated to how early things shut down in small Southern towns. By nine-thirty, most of Rivermist was already in bed, or at least at home in their pajamas. But there was still enough intermittent traffic on the road that the bum she'd almost made roadkill might walk headfirst into oncoming traffic if he weren't careful.

Since he looked about a fifth-of-scotch past sober, careful seemed a long shot.

Grateful she was alone—that she'd just dropped her six-year-old, Mandy, off at a sleepover—she locked her doors and lowered her window enough to talk through the crack.

"Sir, do you need some help?" she asked, pulling alongside him.

"Gotta find Critter," he mumbled, walking right past her in his search for what sounded like a lost pet.

Something in his voice, something about his threadbare plaid coat, seemed oddly familiar.

That in itself was nothing new. Déjà-vu moments lurked behind every corner of this place she'd sworn as a teenager never to return to.

So why was she rolling forward, lowering the window a little more?

"Are you looking for your dog, mister?"

"No, damn it. Got no use for dogs. Crritterrr…" he groused, stumbling into her fender, then shuffling off again.

Got no use for dogs.

The phrase churned up more unwanted memories. Another man, sitting on a porch swing, had said exactly the same thing to her when she was a little girl. He'd been holding a cat named—

"Critter?" she said out loud. "Mr. Cain?"

It was hard to tell, looking through the darkness and the unkempt hair that partially hid his face. But as she drove closer and set the hand brake, the resemblance was unmistakable.

"Mr. Cain!" She rolled the window the rest of the way down and grabbed him by the arm. *Good Lord.* "Mr. Cain, Critter's been dead for over ten years."

"What?" He rounded on her. Bleary, bloodshot eyes glared. "Who are you, and what the hell do you know about my Critter?"

"It's me. Jennifer Gardner."

The man who used to jokingly refer to her as his daughter didn't recognize her. Little wonder. His and her father's friendship hadn't survived the first year after Neal's sentencing. It was as if he hadn't been able to look at her anymore, or spend time in her home, with her parents. With anyone, really.

"I was there when you and Neal buried Critter, remember?" she prompted.

"What?" A tear trickled down his cheek, breaking her heart. "Critter's dead?"

She pulled to the shoulder and got out. Hurried to his side, the frigid night air blasting away at the lingering warmth from the Honda's rattling heater. "It's freezing out here. Why don't I take you home? You'll feel better in the morning."

"No!" From the smell of his breath, beer had been his best friend tonight, not scotch. He wiped his eyes and looked wildly about. "I've got to find Critter."

She steadied him as he stumbled, steering him toward the car. "Why don't we check your house? Critter's probably waiting at the back door, wondering why you're not there to let her in."

"You think so?" Hope spread like sunshine across his face, pushing away the sick pallor of too much alcohol and years of dissipation. "You think she went home?"

"I bet she's there now, crying for her dinner. Why don't we get her some milk?" Jenn opened the passenger door and turned him until he fell backward into the car. He cursed when he bumped his head on the way down.

"Critter loves milk. That's what Wanda started giving her when she was just a kitten. Critter was always Wanda's cat." His voice roughened, and his tears made a return appearance at the mention of his long-dead wife. "I've gotta take care of her. I promised Wanda."

Jenn made sure his arms and legs were out of the way and shut the door. Shivering, she slid behind the wheel and reached over to secure his seat belt. "Don't worry, Mr. Cain. We'll take care of Critter."

"You've always been such a good girl." He patted her hand. Then seconds later, he began to snore.

Wealthy, indomitable Nathan Cain, the Howard Hughes of Rivermist, was sleeping it off in her car. Her heart turned over as she absorbed his deteriorated condition.

It was an unwritten rule that she and her father never discussed the Cain family, not after her parents' final falling out with Nathan only a few months after Neal's conviction. And she hadn't exactly pushed the issue since moving home for the first time since she'd run away at seventeen. She and her dad had enough to deal with, just trying to learn to live together again. They didn't interact with or discuss the Comptons, either, except for the odd run-ins she kept having with Bobby's younger brother, Jeremy.

All that avoiding took a buttload of work in a town this size. Only in Mr. Cain's case, it had been easy. He'd been holed up in his empty mansion for years, she'd heard, grieving his son, angry at the world. But nowhere near as angry, she knew from personal experience, as he probably was at himself.

And she of all people hadn't even bothered to stop by and check on him. She glanced at the bum beside her. Panic attacked as swiftly as the rush of shame. She couldn't look at Nathan Cain, she realized, even in his current condition, and not see Neal.

Cut it out! Give the smelly man a ride home, and be done with it.

Squaring her shoulders, sliding the heat lever to High, she checked for oncoming traffic and made a U-turn across the center line. The Cain place was at the other end of town, amidst the avenue of homes that had been built before the Civil War, yet some- home survived destruction.

No doubt her dad would still be up, keeping track of her comings and goings as carefully as he had her last year at home as a teenager—the year she'd been hell-bent on destroying her and her parents' lives. The year before she'd ditched the memories and the nightmares, and everyone who came along with them.

He would want to know why she was home late. There'd be no point in dodging his questions. By morning, Rivermist would be abuzz about her giving the town pariah a ride home. Heaven knew how the news would spread at this late hour, but it would. And Reverend Gardner was going to freak.

But easing Mr. Cain's mind about a long-dead cat was the least she could do for this man she'd run from the longest. A man who'd lost everything and, just as she had for too long, chosen to give up.

CHAPTER TWO

"No," NEAL BARKED over the cell phone, about twenty minutes before the butt crack of dawn. "I don't want anyone talking with Edgar Martinez but me. I'll be there in half an hour to go over your notes. But I'm taking the meeting."

He'd be there in half an hour? Since when did Stephen Creighton get into the office first?

Since Neal had started falling further and further behind, his everyday caseload turning into one unheard-of delay after another. Since he couldn't sleep, couldn't focus, from thinking about the nonconversation he'd had two weeks ago with a certain Dr. Wilber Harden. Then Nathan had hung up on him the one time Neal had gotten through to the man over the phone, saying nothing but a few choice curses.

And what did Neal have to show for the aggravation? Finishing his Friday morning run with the added bonus of the wet-behind-his-ears lawyer he'd hired a year ago chewing on his ass.

"I don't know what's going on, man," Stephen

said, taking another bite. "This case is a no-brainer. If you don't have time for it, let me take over. Edgar Martinez—"

"Martinez is my problem until he goes to trial. And if I thought it was a no-brainer, I would have advised him to settle."

"The D.A.'s offer is a gift." Not intimidated by Neal's ex-con rep, Stephen plowed forward where other colleagues treaded more delicately. The kid had the pedigree of a philanthropist, but the guts of a street fighter. Neal's kind of guts. "The public defender wanted Edgar to take the plea a week ago."

"It's a crap offer, and we're not taking it." Neal's legal-aid center, funded first by his mother's exceptionally well-invested money, then by grants and donations from several silent partners from Atlanta's legal community, had become the bane of Georgia's prosecutors. He took the cases of people who couldn't afford pricey defense attorneys, and he never plea-bargained until he'd squeezed the last ounce of concession from the district attorney's office.

The best lawyer he'd ever known had taught him that tactic.

"Push too hard on this one," Stephen argued, "and our client's going to end up with no deal at all. This is a county D.A., and he's not taking kindly to being put on hold. Neither is the public defender."

"And Edgar shouldn't take kindly to them rail-roading his son. The public defender wants to plead this one out, to save herself a trip to Statesboro for the court date."

"You don't know that. You won't even take her calls. I have, and—"

"Well, don't! You're making us look anxious to settle, and that cuts me off at the balls. Be ready to bring me up to speed, then stay the hell away from the meeting if you can't stick with the game plan."

Neal ended the call and flipped the cell phone onto the heap of tangled sheets atop his bed, more angry at himself and his increasingly bad mood than anyone else.

Stephen was right. He'd let the Martinez case slide. Meanwhile there was an eighteen-year-old kid sitting in a south Georgia jail, counting on Neal to get him out. Only Neal had spent more time away from the office than he'd been there ever since Buford's call, as he tried to first ignore, and then come to grips with, the reality that his father was sick. Damn sick, even if Doc Harden wouldn't say any more than it was about time Neal up and paid attention to the man.

Oh, he was paying attention all right. He was standing there soaked to the skin from the near-freezing rain outside, his teeth chattering for a hot shower, when where he should have been hours ago was in the office doing the job he did better than anyone else in town.

He kicked off his shoes and peeled out of his sweats. Turning the shower on full blast, he cursed every hour he'd let slip though his fingers since Buford's call. He should have followed up with Martinez days ago. Should have worked out Juan's release, and be pushing for a pre trial settlement the D.A. would hate but be inclined to live with. Whatever it took not to be dragged into court to face the very talented, but anal retentive, Stephen Creighton, who was an ace at slow-playing the proceedings, drawing them out indefinitely, if that's what it took to get their client the best deal.

Neal caught his expression in the mirror gone hazy with shower steam. On the job, he put himself out there one hundred percent. No holding back. He manufactured Hail Mary deals that changed the lives of those people who got snared in the churning cogs of an overburdened legal system. He cut through the bull, found the truth, then hammered away until the courts bent to his will.

Only this time, instead of forcing a solution, he'd become part of the problem. One more person Edgar Martinez and his son couldn't trust to put their interests first.

Because the battle he should be fighting wasn't here. And it refused to be dealt with over the phone, no matter much he needed to take care of things long distance. The life he'd made in Atlanta wasn't working anymore. He'd lost his focus and there was no getting it back. Not until he'd dealt with the sick old man, and all the memories that came with him, that Neal no longer had the option of avoiding.

CHAPTER THREE

"YOU CAN'T BE SERIOUS." Joshua Gardner slouched at the kitchen table, taking the news of Jenn's plans to visit Nathan Cain about as well as his granddaughter did a second helping of spinach.

Jenn breathed deeply to steady her resolve, then finished cleaning up after the French toast from Mandy's Saturday breakfast. Out of the corner of her eye, she watched her father shift restlessly in his age-worn chair. Conflict didn't suit the good reverend. It kinda bit, then, that she'd been rattling his views of the world and his faith since she was sixteen.

He was trying to make her being back work, she'd give him that. And the effort was far more than she'd expected.

"I can't ignore what I saw any longer." She turned to the pantry and plucked boxes of macaroni and cheese and instant soup from the lined shelves, making a mental grocery list of what she'd need to replace. "How anyone in this town can look at that lonely old man and not do whatever they can to help him is beyond me. The least people can do is make sure he has something to eat. I'm taking him some food. What's the harm in that?"

She'd spent two weeks trying to forget. Had accepted her father's silence as a warning to avoid the topic entirely for the sake of preserving the peace. But the reality of Nathan Cain's disheveled appearance and deplorable hygiene, and the sty of a kitchen she'd glimpsed when she'd helped him through his rotted-out back door, refused to be ignored any longer.

"The people in this town tried to help him, Jenn. He's made it more than clear he isn't interested. The man disowned his own son while the boy was still in prison, he wanted to be left alone so badly."

"And that makes how he's living all right?"

"No," her father boomed in an uncharacteristic shout. "It makes it *his* choice."

They hadn't talked about faith and religion since she was a kid, but her father still held tightly to the beliefs that had stopped comforting her years ago. Beliefs so totally contradicted by his continued rift with his former best friend, Jenn bit her tongue to keep from calling him on it. Having it out with her father about a long-dead relationship that didn't matter anymore held the appeal of a bikini wax.

Except it did matter. After seeing Nathan again,

how could it not? Even if helping him meant letting in more memories that she could frankly do without.

"Nathan's exactly where he wants to be," her dad said, inching a bit closer to his calm, reasonable self. "Alone. If he wants to live the life of a bum, leave him be."

"If you'd only seen how terrible that house looked…."

A spark of concern flashed across her dad's face, erased all too quickly by a wince of resignation that turned her stomach. She'd had her part in these two men's estrangement. A starring role.

"I don't think you should be going over there." Salt-and-pepper grayed his dark hair now. A flurry of lines were etched across his fifty-five-year-old face, helped along by recent bypass surgery. "And I don't think it's appropriate for Mandy to go with you. Why not leave her home with me?"

Because, I'm not putting my daughter in the middle of our problems any more than she already is.

"Are you worried about Mandy because Mr. Cain's a drunk and hasn't been to church in years?" she asked. "Or because us being seen there will start even more talk around town?"

"Is it so terrible that I'm concerned what people think about my granddaughter? This is a small town. I'm the pastor of a conservative congregation. I'm just asking for a little discretion while the two of you settle in."

If only his concern were that simple.

"We've been back for three months, Dad. We're as settled as we're going to be." Jenn counted the buttons down the front of his oxford shirt. Anything but looking him in the eye. Nathan wasn't the only man she'd become a pro at avoiding. "Mandy has the town eating out of her hands. I'm the one you're worried about, and we both know it."

Silence was her father's only response, when she'd give her world for an encouraging *you know I trust you, honey*.

Her teenage tantrums and public antics—her determination to burn through the pain and the loneliness after Neal's conviction until she'd felt nothing at all—had turned her father into this careful, cautious man. Because of her, he'd become the patron saint of playing it safe.

She'd come back after all these years to help, because he'd asked her to. He'd actually called her after his heart attack and asked for help. She'd been blown away, and determined to do things right this time. Mandy and her grandfather deserved this chance to know each other. But running into Nathan had shown her there was a limit to how much *playing it safe* she could stomach, how much confrontation she could avoid and still live with herself.

She crossed her arms and stared down both her father and her moment of truth.

"I'm doing everything I can not to make waves for you again," she said. "But—"

"Grandpa, Grandpa!" Mandy flew into the kitchen, a colorful bundle of creative energy dressed in the pink and lime-green overalls Jenn had bought in the dead of winter, because they made her think of lemonade and watermelon on a summer afternoon. "Grandpa, guess what!"

The six-year-old hovered in front of the table, her hands braced on her grandfather's knees. If it weren't for Jenn's careful instructions that Grandpa wasn't to be jostled or bumped, the child no doubt would have launched herself into his lap.

"What?" Jenn's father smiled down at the living miniature of both his daughter and his late wife.

Green eyes sparkling, golden hair pulled back in a curling ponytail, Mandy held up a wrinkled sheet of paper covered in unintelligible hieroglyphics. "I wrote a letter to read to Grandma tonight."

He took the paper. Ran a shaking hand across its surface.

"Grandma's gone, sweetheart. She's gone to heaven."

Jenn blinked at the sound of her father's grief for the high-school sweetheart he'd lost to breast cancer just three years ago.

"Mommy reads my letters to God when I say my prayers," Mandy replied in a stage whisper. Her hand cupped her mouth as she leaned forward to share her secret. "She says He passes my letters on to Grandma."

Jenn's dad looked at her over her daughter's head. He set the letter aside and hugged Mandy. He started to speak, swallowed, then cleared his throat. "Amanda Grace, I know how much you want to talk with Grandma—"

"I wish I'd met her before she left for heaven." Mandy's head dropped. "Mommy says she would have liked me."

"Of course she would have. And I'm sure she wishes she'd met you, too." He waited for Mandy to look up. Then his grandfatherly understanding rearranged itself into the earnest gaze of Reverend Joshua Gardner, champion of finding spiritual meaning from any and every situation. "But as much as we want to talk to the loved ones we've lost, we need to remember what our prayers are supposed to be for."

"But—"

"Our talking time with God shouldn't be about Grandma," he said with a gentle firmness that had won countless souls.

Jenn couldn't believe what she was hearing.

He produced a smile she was certain he didn't

feel, then tried to give Mandy another hug. Her stiff little body refused to melt into him this time.

"Grandma's happy in heaven," he said. "God's taking excellent care of her, so we can stop worrying."

"But Mommy said God talks to Grandma for me." Mandy pulled away, planting her hands on her little girl hips. "She said—"

"Sweetie." Jenn turned her by the shoulders. "Go find your shoes and put them on. Mommy needs to be on time for her Teens in Action meeting."

Dragging her feet, shooting her grandfather an exasperated, why-won't-you-ever-listen look, the deflated child walked from the room, her letter trailing from her hand.

Olivia Gardner's funeral had been Jenn's first visit back to Rivermist after she left as a pregnant runaway—and it had only been a day-trip at that. She had found a way to mourn the loss of her mother, as well as the years they hadn't had together. But she would send singing telegrams heavenward if that's what it took to give her child as much of the grandmother she'd never known as she could.

She waited until Mandy was out of earshot, then she rounded on her father.

"Lay off, Dad."

"I was only—"

"You were turning something special to Mandy into a potshot at my parenting choices."

"That's not fair." His gaze didn't quite meet hers.

"Neither is telling a six-year-old she can't write letters to her dead grandmother."

"The letters are fine, but—"

"*But* nothing." There always had to be a but. "If you have a problem with what I'm teaching Mandy, take it up with me."

"I've accepted that your ideas about religion and spirituality are more liberal than mine now." The way he said *liberal* had visions of defrocked televangelists swimming through Jenn's mind. "But I won't apologize for believing differently in my own home."

"I never asked you to apologize." She made herself stand a bit taller, when a younger Jenn would have sunk into a nearby chair and pretended not to care. *He was right. She was wrong. Dangerously familiar territory.* "But when I moved home, you agreed to let me make my own decisions about raising my daughter. And so far, you've done a lousy job of it. You have to stop interfering. Stop the passive-aggressive criticizing every time you don't agree with my decisions."

"So, just like when you turned up pregnant at seventeen, I'm supposed to happily accept how you choose to live your life?"

"No. I never expected you to be happy about it." The cleansing breath she took froze in lungs that weren't the least bit interested. "*Happy* went out the window when you demanded I put my unborn baby up for adoption."

His shock echoed in the silence separating them. They never talked about that final argument. Ever.

"There was more to it than that," he said, "and you know it."

"The sentiment's the same, however you look at it. You didn't approve of me then, and you don't approve of me now."

He pushed up from the table, announcing the end of their conversation by heading slowly into the den. He was steadier on his feet every day, but he still looked so very tired.

For the first time Jenn followed, pursuing instead of backing down. She hadn't been ready for this conversation at seventeen. But at twenty-four, she was a pro at managing the past without falling back into it. Rebuilding instead of destroying. Healing.

"I know I messed up before I got pregnant with Mandy." She closed her eyes at the memory of the drugs, the parties, the mindless need to escape. "And I know my running away hurt you and Mom terribly. But I did what I had to do." She'd worked two and three jobs to pay for child care while she put herself through night school. Earned scholarships—whatever it took. "And whether or not you condone how I've accomplished it, I created a good life for me and my daughter. I've done everything I can to make up for my mistakes."

"Yes, by working in that women's health center in North Carolina, where they dispense free condoms and birth control pills and perform abortions for teenagers without parental consent." It was a sanctimonious speech. He looked as if he were having as hard a time swallowing it as she was. "You're enabling other young women to make the same easy mistakes you did, or worse."

"Easy?" People who saw women making the kinds of life-changing, life-or-death decisions Jenn had as "getting off easy," needed to work a month in a free clinic and then get back to her. "A women's health center is the only reason I survived after I ran away. I was sick and alone, and Mandy came two months premature. We both would have died without that center. Trust me, nothing about the experience was easy."

He glanced at his shifting feet. "Your mother and I never meant for you to be at risk. We always wanted you to be here, to be safe. We did what we thought was best."

"Well, your way wasn't best. Not for me." Her raised hand stopped his next sentence. "But none of that matters anymore. I'm happy to help you get back on your feet. And I'd love for Mandy to grow up in Rivermist. But we can't stay if you won't stop interfering with the decisions I make for her. And, whether you approve or not, I can't not do what I think is right for Nathan Cain."

"Even if I know where the mistakes you're making are leading you?" Uncertainty weighted each word with the kind of doubt that was so out of character it gave her hope.

"You have to let me make my own way, Dad." Her fingers itched with a child's urge to hug his neck. "My own mistakes."

Give me a chance.

Just one more chance.

"I'm not sure how to do that."

A familiar sadness speared her heart. When it came to choosing between trust and responsibility, trust had come in second with her and her father since that night of the homecoming dance, when the sheriff called to say that she and Neal were at the police station.

"Mommy?" Mandy called from the foyer.

Jenn sighed and grabbed her purse off her parents' paisley-printed couch.

"Don't worry, I'm dropping Mandy off at her friend Ashley's on my way to the Teens in Action meeting." She led a group of local kids who attended her father's church, a role in his church he'd never fully supported. "I'll stop by Nathan's before I pick her up, and we'll be home around two. I want us to stay here with you, Dad." It surprised her even as she said it just how much. "And I'm willing to meet you halfway. The rest is up to you."

Forcing her legs to move, she fought not to take back the closest thing to an ultimatum she'd ever given her father.

"Let's go, punkin." She knelt in the foyer to tie one of Mandy's forever dangling shoelaces, laying aside the bags of food she'd packed for another father— the father of the boy who'd left a lifetime ago and taken a piece of both her and Nathan's hearts with him.

She stuffed her daughter into the heavy coat Georgia's mild climate made necessary only in the very dead of winter, and ushered her out the front door. January wind blasted their faces. Just the ticket to keep Jenn's mind off the young boy she'd planned to spend the rest of her life with, here in this beautiful, historic town that—without him in it—might never feel like home again.

Her parents and their disapproval weren't the only reasons she'd stayed away. And her dad's estrangement from Nathan Cain wasn't the only regret that had kept her from facing the Cain house and Nathan's misery.

There was too much of Neal still here. So much more than should still be able to touch her. Emotional ties to an idealistic past she'd thought she'd put behind her. Did he know about her? Did he even know about his own father?

Stop it!

She helped her daughter into the car. The beautiful child whose creation had been Jenn's rock-bottom. The child who had also been the reason she'd finally taken a stab at living, rather than praying for an end.

She started the car's cold engine. Neal was gone, and she was here, trying to carve out a new beginning. To live the life she had now, rather than wallowing in the past she couldn't undo. Isn't that what she'd just finished telling her father she wanted? Why she was headed for the Cain place later today?

Memories or no memories, she had a job to do. She couldn't turn her back on Neal's father any more than she had on her own.

Better than anyone in Rivermist, she understood the pain still ripping at Nathan Cain. Pain she was more than a little responsible for. A responsibility that she wouldn't ignore a single day longer just because she couldn't handle remembering the boy her heart would never let go of completely, no matter how many miles and years separated them now.

CHAPTER FOUR

"JENN, YOU'VE HAD BOYFRIENDS, right?" Traci Carpenter asked over the plate of fries she and Jenn were devouring. At seventeen, Traci probably saw Jenn's twenty-four years as so far over the hill, boyfriends would be a distant memory.

"It's been a while." So much for putting Neal Cain out of her mind. "But I think I remember boys."

The church's youth activity that weekend was a trip to Freddy's, Jenn's favorite place to eat in Rivermist. She was the leader of this sprawling band of youth and energy, so she got to pick where they met. Freddy's had a laser jukebox, cheap junk food and plenty of booths for the teenagers to commandeer. The perfect way to kill a few hours before a handful of the kids had to dress for that afternoon's varsity basketball games.

She'd volunteered to revamp the church's floundering Saturday activities after it had become clear there was no chaperoned place Rivermist's teens would be caught dead hanging out in. The church leaders, fresh out of creative ideas, had agreed to let Jenn give it a try—as a lay leader only, they'd tripped all over themselves to point out.

Now under her leadership, the kids were opening up to the idea of being part of a crowd that had something more constructive to do than cruising or partying the weekend away. And the satisfaction of working with them had Jenn hooked in a way she should have seen coming.

Traci Carpenter had been shadowing Jenn for a couple of Saturdays now. Always there, always angling to sit closer. Always the last one hanging around when things wrapped up. The signals weren't that tough to read. The girl had something to say, something to talk about. She just hadn't worked up the nerve before now.

"So, how long did it take before your boyfriends…" The teen twisted the straw in her milk shake. At Traci's insistence, she and Jenn were sitting several booths away from the rest of the kids. "I mean, once you'd gone together for six months or so…"

"Haven't you and Brett Hamilton been dating for a lot longer than six months?" Jenn swiped a fry through the ketchup, using her best girlfriend voice. At least she was pretty sure that's how girlfriends gossiping about boys sounded.

"This isn't about me and Brett." Crimson flooded Traci's cheeks.

"Of course not."

"I have this friend," Traci whispered. "And she's seeing this older guy. You know, older. More sophisticated."

The fry halfway to Jenn's mouth stalled. "And… your friend and this sophisticated guy are doing what, exactly?"

"Well, you know…." The girl's nonchalance clashed with the way she nervously kicked the table leg between them. Blond and blue-eyed, she was wearing a high-fashion ensemble no doubt bought on one of her mother's shopping excursions to Atlanta. "What do you think they're doing?"

Jenn popped the fry into her mouth. Kept her expression free of anything but casual interest. The label of church leader fit her social-worker training like a sweater shrunk once too often in the dryer. But giving teenagers a back door into discovering what they believed was right up her alley.

This conversation, if nothing else today, she could handle like a pro.

Another look across the restaurant, and Traci leaned closer. "So, some of the girls and I were wondering. If my friend needed some advice, or maybe something like birth control, or…whatever…could she come to you?"

Jenn silently processed the complications and conflicts this conversation was headed for. *Informa-*

tion, she reminded herself. *Never make a decision without all the information you can get your hands on.*

She cleared her throat. "Can your friend talk with her parents?"

"Not about stuff like this. Her parents are stuck in the dark ages. They'd never let her see this guy if they knew how old he is."

"How much older are we talking?"

"He's in college." The plate of fries was the only thing Traci would look at now. "Well, he was."

"He graduated?"

"Not…not exactly. He dropped out."

Of course they were talking about Traci and not a friend, and her "older guy" was probably in his early twenties at most. But it still sounded as if she'd set herself up for some huge disappointments if Mr. Wonderful didn't pan out. And something already had the girl worried. Teens didn't just up and talk to adults about stuff like sex and protection. Jenn never had when she'd been in Traci's shoes, not until it was too late.

"I'm not sure how much I can help your friend, since I don't know her," she reasoned out loud. "But I do know what I'd tell you or any of my girls if I learned you were getting into a relationship like the one you're describing."

Defensiveness crept across Traci's expression. "If

you're going to tell me that good girls wait and that I'm…that my friend's going to hell if she doesn't, don't bother. I've heard it all before."

"No, I'd be the last person to preach that to you."

Qualifying what it meant to be *good* was one of the most overused weapons adults wielded. Guilt and recrimination didn't get the job done. That kind of moral certainty pushed kids away, instead of teaching them to honor themselves and the responsibility that goes along with making their own decisions.

When she'd been Traci's age, hadn't she gone out of her way to do the exact opposite of her parents' by-the-book vision for her life? Culminating in getting herself pregnant in an alcohol-induced haze with a boy she couldn't even remember.

Honesty. Information. Trust.

That's what Traci needed from someone. And it looked as if Jenn had just been volunteered.

"I'd ask a good friend like you to be very careful." She weighed each word before she said it. "Teenage boys, even older guys, don't always see relationships the same way teenage girls do."

"He's not just interested in sex." Freckles stood out in sharp contrast with the flush spreading down Traci's neck. "He's not that kind of guy. It's just that…"

"All I'm saying is that he might not have as much

at stake in this as your friend does. I'd want her to think carefully before she did anything she couldn't take back."

"And if she's already thought it through?"

Traci's certainty geared Jenn into action. "And she doesn't want to talk with her parents?"

"Not a chance."

"Then your friend has to protect herself. I'd like to have the chance to talk with her. Very real consequences come with what she's doing. But nothing's more important than making sure she protects herself."

"What…what if her guy doesn't want to use protection?"

"That's a deal-breaker, sweetie." Jenn's hands curled into fists above her knees. She was advising the only child of one of her father's senior deacons about safe sex. Nothing like jumping off a cliff without a parachute.

But conversations like this were exactly why she'd chosen the work she did. They were unpredictable. Priceless. Life-changing.

"That would leave you…" she began. "It would leave your friend unprotected from infectious disease. Things like AIDS."

"What about the pill?"

"The pill doesn't protect you from disease, Traci."

"But, what if he's sure he's clean?"

"What if he's lying?" Jenn managed not to snort. Barely.

"He's not."

"How can you be sure?"

"He says he's never been with anyone but her, okay!" Traci pulled her legs up, drew her knees to her chest and locked her arms around them. "He says she's his first."

"And you believe him?" Jenn blurted out before her brain overcame her shock at the girl's naiveté.

Her social-worker mojo couldn't have picked a worse time to bail.

"Fine. Forget I asked." Traci scooted to the edge of the booth.

"Wait." Jenn caught hold of her arm. "I'm sorry, all right? But you've got to admit, you've laid an awful lot on me for a Saturday lunch at Freddy's. Give me a chance here."

Tension trembled down Traci's arm.

"I don't want to see you or your friend get hurt," Jenn pressed. "And if you weren't a little worried about that happening, why did you come to me for advice?"

"Are you saying you'll help me?" The teenager looked every bit the scared seventeen-year-old she didn't want to be. "You'll help me, and you won't tell my folks?"

"So, we *are* talking about you. Not a friend?"

"Yeah." Traci's head dropped. She slid back into the booth.

"But we're not talking about Brett?" Jenn's stomach churned.

"No." Traci shook her head and stared at her lap. "He still thinks…I mean, everyone still thinks we're together. But it's over."

"Then why are you still dating him?"

"This other guy, he lives in another town. It's not like we can get together here. If I broke up with Brett, how would I explain where I've been when I…you know…"

"When you're with your other guy?" This upstanding, almost virginal college dropout who was letting Traci lie and sneak around, but who only had her best interest at heart.

"I…I'm afraid to keep sleeping with him without protection, but my mom knows every doctor in town, and he doesn't like condoms." Traci's expression begged Jenn to see the sense in her desperate, messed-up logic.

"So you're already having unprotected sex." Jenn held her breath and hoped for a miracle. "For how long?"

"A month—" Traci picked lint from the paper napkin she'd wadded into a ball "—maybe two."

It was all too obvious, suddenly, what they were really talking about.

"When was your last period, Traci?"

Tears welled in the teenager's eyes.

Well, damn.

"Have you taken a home pregnancy test?"

"N-no." Traci wiped at her eyes. Chewed on the corner of her mouth. "I…I didn't want to…"

"You didn't want to know?"

If only blissful ignorance were as effective as prophylactics.

"Are you going to help me?" the teenager asked, her voice full of a little girl's fear. "I don't know what to do. And I thought you of all people would…you know, understand. Will you help me?"

Contradicting impulses left Jenn speechless while she did some of the fastest thinking of her life. If she tried to talk Traci into going to her parents, she'd lose this battle before it began. That was a discussion for another time, when the girl didn't already look ready to bolt for the door. She could tell the Carpenters herself, but to the teen that would be the worst kind of betrayal. And that would blow Jenn's shot at damage control.

And let's not forget my father and my sparkling new fresh start. And what he and his congregation would expect her to do as the sensible, conservative, levelheaded leader she'd agreed to be when she'd taken the volunteer position with the church's teens.

Helping Traci on her own meant breaking the

trust of everyone around her. Keeping the girl's secret, even for a few days, might cost Jenn a whole lot more than her job working with Teens in Action.

But none of that could compete with keeping the girl and her baby safe. And if Jenn were the only adult Traci was asking for guidance, that meant the next words out of her mouth could only be—

"Of course I'll help." She covered Traci's hand with her own. "I'll do whatever I can, on one condition. You leave the door open to talking with your parents."

"If you tell them, I'll run away. I can move in with my guy anytime I want—"

"I'm not going to tell anyone anything. But you might need to, if—"

"Jenn, Traci." Brett Hamilton headed toward them from the other side of the restaurant. "We've got to get ready for the game."

Giving her watch an annoyed glance, Jenn squeezed Traci's hand. "I'm going to set up an appointment for you with a friend of mine who works in the free clinic in Colter. I'll get you in first thing Monday. They open at ten."

Traci pulled her hand away as the all-state center she'd gone steady with since freshmen year drew closer.

"Promise me you'll keep the appointment." Jenn scribbled her cell number on a napkin and shoved it into the teenager's hand, in case the girl had lost the card she'd given all the kids their first Saturday together. "You can call me anytime you need to. I'll even take you to the clinic if you want."

Traci glanced nervously at Brett.

"Promise me you'll see the doctor," Jenn pressed. "We have to be sure—"

"Okay, I promise." Traci shoved the napkin into her jacket pocket a second before Brett reached their table. "But I'll go myself."

"You ready?" Brett gave Traci's cheek a noisy kiss.

"Yeah." Traci edged around him and headed for the door without looking back.

With a wink and a shrug for Jenn, Brett trailed after her.

Jenn lagged behind as the kids paired up and piled back into their cars. She paid her bill and tried to swallow the bitter taste of French fries and foreboding. Just once, couldn't she catch a break in this town?

Some in the church had been concerned, her father had said, when she'd taken on the floundering teen group.

Concerned.

After all, given her history, was she really the kind of person they wanted influencing their impressionable children? The facts were what they were.

She'd been a runaway. An unwed teen mother. She was only a slightly older version of the girl who'd turned to the parties and addictions to obliterate the self-hatred and emptiness she'd only made worse. She'd destroyed her relationship with her parents and had almost cost her father his church.

She'd come back home determined to live down her past and make a fresh start for her daughter's sake. Now with one simple offer to help a reckless teenager who reminded her too much of herself at seventeen, she was angling for trouble all over again. The kind of trouble that made being seen taking a few bags of food to Nathan Cain a nonissue.

Wrestling open the rusted door of her car, she slid inside and stared at the picturesque world on the other side of the windshield. Fought the childish urge to pick up Mandy at Ashley's and drive away from Rivermist and the past that seemed incapable of letting her go.

She'd felt a shining moment of strength when she'd stood up to her father that morning. With a snort, she pulled out onto North Street and headed for the Cain place. Had she really grown up and grown stronger over the last seven years, or had she simply gotten better at faking it?

NOW ENTERING RIVERMIST, GEORGIA, the faded sign read in the midday sun. The same faded, beaten-up sign that had been there for as long as Neal could remember.

He was hands down the most *unwelcome* person to ever enter Rivermist. But somewhere between his apartment and the office that morning, he'd accepted the inevitable. He had to make sure his father was all right. It was time to settle things with the man and this place. So Stephen had taken the Martinez meeting solo after all, and Neal had settled for a soul-searching, two-hour detour down I-75 South.

A part of him hated Nathan for making him care this much again. Another, desperate part needed to see the old man so badly it made no sense. Nothing good could come from letting himself be sucked back into this place. He'd bet his restored '65 Mustang GT Fastback on it—one of the few luxuries he'd indulged in since regaining control of his trust fund.

Neal winced.

He'd been so certain staying away the last three years was the right thing. Most of him still was. But what if…

Damn.

There was no room in his world for *what-ifs*. He'd finally accepted his mistakes and he'd moved on. He'd been determined that as much good as possible would come from Bobby's death, his prison sentence and the lives both had shattered. *What-if* wasn't going to make that happen. But second thoughts had hounded him the entire drive over.

Medical what-ifs—all likely candidates for a man his father's age—that Doc Harden hadn't confirmed nor denied. What the cranky old doctor *had* said repeatedly was that Neal should get his black-sheep self home and ask his father what was going on in person.

Neal shoved the transmission into Reverse. Gripping the steering wheel, he fantasized about banking into a steep turn and barreling back to Atlanta and the people he actually could help. Then with a curse, he yanked the gearshift back to Neutral and set the hand brake.

Nathan had refused any but the most basic medical intervention for whatever ailed him. Maybe Neal could talk his father into doing more, the doctor had suggested.

Maybe.

The one useless thing Neal despised more than *what-if.*

His life was about cold, hard reality. No more destructive emotions. No grand gestures. No time for wishing things were different or looking back to what had been. Now *maybe* had brought him to a screeching halt on the outskirts of town, unable to keep going for more reasons than just Nathan.

"Jennifer Gardner."

There. He'd said her name, and it hadn't hurt a bit.

She'd no doubt moved away years ago. Gotten on with a life that could never have included him. She'd have missed him. Mourned for him. But she'd have moved on by now. And that's what he'd wanted for her, why he'd refused to answer the letters she'd written to him in prison. Thirty of them in all. Precious ties to the beautiful girl he'd once loved. Letters still kept in the back of his bedroom closet.

Unopened.

Unread.

Impossible to throw away.

With the discipline that came from years of practice, he refused to let her face materialize in his mind. But as always, the perfection of her crystal-clear laugh haunted him.

What if she was still in Rivermist...

With a curse, he revved the idling Ford engine, hating the rush of helplessness that came with the sound. Only a coward would turn back now, but that's exactly what his instincts told him to do.

Run.

Run just one more time, and leave these people in peace.

Flipping his hometown's welcome sign the bird, he revved the motor again. But he stayed put, same as before. Not able to move forward or head back.

The man he'd become didn't run. He fought until he found a way to get through whatever was facing him.

So why did the reality of finally being back here have him spinning his wheels and going absolutely nowhere?

CHAPTER FIVE

FACING THE CAIN kitchen door and the layer of rust covering its outer screen, Jenn mentally counted backward to her last tetanus shot. A ridiculous excuse for stalling, but now that she was here, she needed time. Just a moment to shut out Traci's bombshell at lunch and refocus on the next Hallmark moment of her day.

The rickety front door had been locked and no one had answered the bell. So she'd snaked around back through the overgrown yard she'd once turned cartwheels in, and the reality of the run-down place, of all that had been left broken for too long, hit home.

Broken.

What a way to describe the chasm yawning between her and this man she'd once loved like a father. The Cain and Gardner families had shared holidays, birthdays and summer barbecues. Winter ski trips. She and Neal had run with the church youth group while their parents chaperoned—a euphemism for keeping the youngsters out of trouble while the adults acted like kids themselves. Their families had been inseparable, intertwining, planning for a shared future, right up until that night. That awful night.

A blast of wind tugged at her coat and her second thoughts. This wasn't about what they'd had, or what they no longer meant to each other. This was about helping Nathan Cain now. Spending a few minutes letting him know someone still cared. Just a few minutes. Was that too much to ask?

She pulled back the screen and knocked. After the fifth knock, her dread at seeing Nathan again gave way to concern. She tried to peer through the curtains covering the center window. But there was nothing to see but dust and shadows. Then, from out of nowhere, one of the shadows moved toward her.

She screamed, her bags dropping in a heap on top of her foot.

"Ouch!" She leaned on the door and massaged her foot through her tennis shoe.

Okay! She got it. She wasn't welcome here.

Then the lock clicked and the door jerked away. Her balance shifted forward. Squealing, she tipped into a mountain that smelled of stale beer and way too little personal hygiene.

"Damn it," Nathan Cain grumbled as she righted herself.

He was dressed in the same filthy, torn jeans as the other night. No shirt, no socks, nothing to combat the morning temperatures. His blond, gray-streaked hair stuck out in more directions than should be possible in a three-dimensional world. And his brown eyes, so dark they were almost black, were swollen and bloodshot. One of his grimy hands lifted to block the afternoon sun.

He still wasn't exactly sober.

"What the hell are you doin' here at the crack of dawn?" groused the man who'd once led Jenn's junior-high Sunday school class. "I've got a good mind to—"

"I—It's one o'clock in the afternoon, Mr. Cain." The stench of him made it difficult to speak. "I—I—"

"I, what?" He gave her a vague perusal, then a twisted smile. "Well, if it isn't little miss Jennifer Gardner. Thought I'd seen the last of you when you sprinted out of here weeks ago."

"I—I wanted to bring a few things over…." She bent to gather the scattered groceries. "I mean, when I dropped you off, the—the kitchen, it looked so…"

Repulsive?

She stooped and reached for a box of macaroni and cheese. Nathan's hand made it there first. Hers recoiled before she could stop herself.

He crouched beside her and handed her the box.

"What business is it of yours what my kitchen looks like?" he asked in little more than a whisper, as if talking in a normal tone hurt.

"I—I just want to help." She stood and put the distance she needed between them, a bag of store-bought guilt hanging from each hand. "Just trying to help a friend."

"Friend?" He straightened, too, his knees cracking, his balance wavering, until all six foot three of him loomed over her. He half collapsed against the door-frame and crossed his arms over his chest. "What gave you the idea I needed help?"

He looked so much like his son even in his run-down state, Jenn caught herself staring.

"I almost ran over you the other night, Mr. Cain. And you didn't— You don't look well."

"Well, isn't that neighborly of you to notice." His stare reinforced his sarcasm.

Then an odd sort of confusion slipped through his antagonism. He inched backward into the house, his motions unnaturally slow. Gone was the grace and co-ordination of the man who'd once given the teenag-ers in town a run for their money on the basketball court.

"If you'll excuse me," he said, manners from another time making a brief appearance. "I'm in the middle of something…something important."

He began closing the door.

"But the groceries." She shuffled the bags to one hand and laid a palm on the door, knowing that pushing him was a bad idea, but completely unable to stop. "I was thinking I could cook you something. Eating might help you feel a little better."

"I feel just fine. And you've got no business here."

His soulless eyes flicked from her hand to the pitying frown she hadn't swallowed fast enough. She was staring at the closed door before she could say another word. Without a second thought, she turned the knob and pushed the door back open.

Nathan was standing in the middle of the kitchen, a can of beer in his hand. He didn't look a bit surprised at her intrusion. He didn't even look angry. Instead, he tipped the can back, happily on his way to inebriation.

"You've got no business here." He drained his beer in the time it took him to reach her.

He attempted to shut her out again, but just keeping his hand from slipping off the doorknob seemed to get the better of him. Jenn had plenty of time to scoot farther inside before the door closed. Oblivious, Nathan barreled straight into her.

"Get the hell out of my house!" He jerked away. "Or I'll call the sheriff."

"No, you won't. The sheriff's probably the only person in town you want to see less than me and my father."

Mr. Cain had nearly killed Glenn Hamilton, the former sheriff's deputy who'd arrived at this same door eight years ago with a warrant for Neal's arrest.

That was the last time she'd stepped foot in the Cain house. The last time anyone from Rivermist had.

She juggled her shopping bags, searching for an uncluttered flat surface to set them on. Finding none, she spotted a relatively clean patch of linoleum beneath the wall-mounted phone and dropped the groceries to the floor.

"How can you bring yourself to eat in here?" The place was downright revolting.

"That's none of your business. Now get out." He was no longer yelling, but his eyes had filled with every awful emotion he had a right to feel toward her.

"I can't do that." Another glance around the room, and her resolve to simply drop off the food, reclaim her daughter and head home for a stimulating evening of worrying her heart out about Traci Carpenter evaporated.

The kitchen table seemed as good a place to start as any. She collected a stack of plates covered with half-eaten food and headed for the sink, moving a pile of empty beer cans to make room to work.

"Are you an alcoholic?" she asked over her shoulder.

"Not yet." There was a long pause. "But I'm working on it."

She'd been prying a burnt hamburger off a plate. Dropping it, she whirled to find him guzzling another can of beer.

"That's not funny! You're killing yourself."

"Not exactly." He saluted her with his can. "But close enough."

"What are you saying?" Afraid she already knew the answer, her heart sank.

"I'm saying I want to be left alone."

"Maybe no one else in this town remembers the man you used to be, but I do. And I can't stand to see you living this way, not when I can help." She spotted a pyramid of prescription bottles on the counter across the room and headed toward it.

Nathan followed, stumbling precariously close to the stove. He caught himself and struck out again, marching toward Jenn as she read the name of a narcotic pain reliever off one of the labels.

"Put that down." He yanked the bottle away and threw it across the room. A swipe of his hand sent the rest of the medicine flying. "I still have more money than God. If I wanted things clean, if I wanted a nurse, I'd hire one."

"You are sick." She peered closer, through the booze and the bluster. Her pulse pounded. "Is that what the drinking's all about?"

"I'm not sick!" he shouted, his voice sounding clearer by the second. He stretched himself to his full height, then he gifted her with a creaky bow. "I'm dying."

"Wh-what?"

"I'm dying. And if I want to drink myself into oblivion, or live in a pigsty, or eat off the floor, it's none of your damn business. So kindly take your food and your condescend...condes... Take your pity, and get out of my house!"

Jenn walked back to the sink, choking on her denial. A myriad of images assailed her. The gentle, funny man she'd loved to listen to classical jazz with. The broken man who'd watched his son escorted from the courtroom in handcuffs. The threadbare bum who'd stumbled into her car just two weeks ago, calling for his wife's favorite cat.

Nathan Cain was dying.

Alone.

Oh, Neal. Where are you?

She picked up a crud-encrusted plate that had once been pristine bone china and began scraping, ashamed by the quick getaway she'd planned.

A stick of dynamite couldn't budge her now.

"Stop it!" Mr. Cain shoved the dish from her hands. It fell to the countertop and splintered. Shattered pieces tinkled onto the hardwood floor. "Now look what you've done...those are Wanda's favorite dishes... she's gonna holler to bring the house down when she gets home. You're gonna explain it to her, not me."

He stepped through the broken china on his way to the refrigerator, his mildewed tennis shoes grinding the pieces into the floor.

Jenn picked up the shattered pottery and watched him pull another beer from the nearly-empty fridge, trying to get her head around the idea that the man was expecting his dead wife home any minute.

"Mr. Cain." She tossed the remains of the plate into the trash, where the bits slid off the teetering pile of waste. "Don't you think—"

"Think what?" He looked her in the eye and popped open the can.

"Why don't I make you a cup of coffee?"

"Coffee's not going to fix what ails me, girl." He chugged half the beer in one swallow and wiped his mouth with the back of his hand. "And don't think my brain's so addled you can sweet-talk me into your version of turning lemons into lemonade. I know my wife is dead, damn it! I may be drunk, but I'm not an idiot. Not yet anyway."

"I don't think you're an idiot." She reached deep for the social worker inside her. For the honesty and detachment that made her so good at her job. She gave the filth around her a pointed stare. "What I think is that this place should be hosed down by a Health Department SWAT team."

Nathan's glower threatened to fade into a chuckle. Eyes a shade more interested than intoxicated watched her move about the kitchen. She picked up another plate and scraped a half-burnt frozen pizza into the sink.

"Better yet," she reconsidered, "burning everything and starting over might not be a bad idea."

The man's hoarse laugh warmed her with the sweet touch of yesterday.

"You always were a pistol, you know that?" He finished his beer and threw the not-quite-empty can toward the trash. It bounced once and hit the floor, dregs of alcohol splattering the grease-stained wallpaper as it rolled to a stop. "Get out."

"I want to help you. I think in your heart you want to be helped. Otherwise, no matter how much you'd had to drink, you wouldn't have gotten into my car the other night. You wouldn't have let me in here today. And I'm about the last person in this town still willing to put any effort into caring about you."

"Because you're my *friend*, right?"

"I'd like to be, yes."

He glared at her, then headed back to the fridge for another beer. Popping it, he slid into one of the kitchen chairs as he drank.

"What are you doing here, Jenn?"

She sat, too, ready to own up to the truth.

"I was a part of Neal going to prison." Flashes of Neal's heartbreaking smile replayed in her mind. Memories of how they'd learned to love each other, to find passion where there'd been only friendship before. "If it weren't for me, he never would have gotten into that awful fight with Bobby Compton, and Bobby wouldn't be dead. And you wouldn't have had to watch Neal plead guilty to charges you couldn't stop. You wouldn't have been hiding away here ever since."

"You responsible for my brain tumor, too?" Not a flicker of emotion colored his face. "Why do you want to buy more trouble? The way I hear it, you've had enough of your own to last you a lifetime."

"Yes, I have." The hollowness inside Jenn threatened to consume her. Without missing a beat, she shoved the emotions back and refocused on the job she had to do here. "But we're not talking about me. We're talking about you, sitting in this house, day after day, hating yourself and everyone else in the world. You used to be part of this community. Now no one even knows who you are. No one knows you're sick."

"I don't care what anybody else knows. I haven't wanted a thing from this town for years."

"That's good, 'cause I don't see anyone else beating down your door but me."

"That's true enough," he said with a wry chuckle. A spark of interest lit his bloodshot eyes.

She hid her smile of relief and played the game. "Let's just say I owe you. If you've got to hate someone for what happened to Neal, why not give yourself a break and hate me for a while. Put me to work, let me help you out around here. You can be as grumpy and impossible to get along with as you like."

He thunked his beer to the table. His half-drunk beer, she noticed.

"You want me to let you keep bothering me, because I hate you? You want to come over here and work yourself to death cleaning up this mess, and all I have to do in return is treat you really, really badly?"

"Yep." She crossed her arms and leaned back in her chair.

She was biting off an enormous responsibility. As if tailing Traci Carpenter wasn't enough to keep her busy.

Have you completely lost your mind?

"What's the catch?" Lawyer's eyes drilled her.

Jenn's blood chilled at the suspicion she saw there. Hard work and putting up with his attitude were a small price to pay for the chance to shine a little light back into this man's life. Even if it meant spending more time in this place, with the past echoing even closer now that she was inside.

"The catch is, you have to start taking care of yourself." She gave him her negotiating face. Every social worker had one. "And the drinking stops. Where are you going to find a better deal than that?"

He picked up the beer again, eyeing its contents. Then with a wicked grin and a flick of his wrist, he hurled the can toward the trash. Beer sprayed them and the wall, then it seeped onto the floor as the can came to rest.

"It's an idea I could warm up to." He leaned back, crossing his arms in a pose exactly like hers.

"Then we have a deal?"

She refused to wipe at the alcohol trickling down her hair and face. Refused to sink into the denial crying deep inside her. *Nathan Cain couldn't be dying. He just couldn't.* Instead she held out her hand. Each moment here, with memories of Neal lurking from every shadow, would be agony. But she'd find a way to make this work. Just like she'd somehow make sure things worked out for Traci.

What would a few more ghosts from her past hurt? Bring 'em on! She was suddenly spoiling for a fight.

"Deal." He swung his arm wide, clasping her hand in a viselike grip. "Sounds like more fun than I've had in years."

NEAL STARED IN DISBELIEF at the house he'd grown up in. Decay shrouded everything in sight, more than living up to Buford's warning about his father's life-style. His gaze dropped again to the footprints forever preserved in concrete at his feet. Two pairs of footprints, one set large and square, the other smaller and clearly more feminine, left in the drying cement on a steamy summer afternoon years ago.

His and Jenn's last summer together.

The concrete was cracked and weathered with age, just like the rest of the place. Once upon a time, his father had been obsessed with winning the neighborhood association's Yard of the Month award. Now the lawn, once manicured and gently sloping away from the house, was a mass of weeds and anthills. Dead shrubs overflowed the flowerbeds. The spindly skeletons of his mother's prized rose bushes were choking on knee-high crabgrass turned brown by the biting cold.

He walked up the path toward the faded oak door. The house's gray brick looked sturdy enough still. But what used to be midnight-blue trim had mottled under the burden of time and too much sun, its pasty color the perfect accompaniment to the falling-down neglect that permeated everything. The few shutters remaining on the windows listed at odd angles, missing row after row of slats. And the two-story traditional's roof had buckled under years of Georgia heat, warping and blistering in places, cracking off in chunks in others. He reached the top of the front steps, avoided several loose boards and turned to survey the yard again.

An unexpected urgency swamped him. Guilt spiked through the need not to be there. The years of silence between him and his father were supposed to have brought the man closure. The peace neither of them had been able to find with the other still in his life. From the looks of things, Nathan had chosen to give up instead.

The chill of the doorknob felt strange as he turned it. Foreign. Unfamiliar. Even stranger when it resisted and refused to pivot.

The door was locked.

As far back as he could remember, his parents had never locked up. There'd been no need in a town like Rivermist. More to the point, he had no keys. He'd thrown them away the day his personal effects were returned when he left prison. He couldn't keep the keys and not want to come back.

But leaving his home behind and being locked out of it were two different things.

"Come on!" He jiggled the handle, then rapped his knuckles on one of the glass panels set in the top half of the custom-built door. He rang the bell, as if that would convince the town recluse to answer.

A shadow behind the frosted glass caught his eye. Someone was coming after all. Someone too tiny and far too feminine-looking, even through the door's grimy windows, to be his father.

Buford had said the man lived alone.

So who the hell was unlocking the front door?

CHAPTER SIX

THE DEADBOLT SCRAPED BACK. The door squeaked open. Hinges made their grinding protest heard. Then everything that should have been gone from Neal's empty heart stood before him, confusion and shock clouding her beautiful features.

Jennifer Gardner.

The embodiment of all he'd given up. The dream it had been pointless to keep dreaming.

His Jennifer.

No! Not his. Not for eight long years.

"What—what are you doing here, Jenn?" He forced out the shorter version of her name. The one he'd never used, not once, after they started dating in high school.

High school.

The memories came rushing back, now that she was standing there in front of him.

They'd fallen in love freshman year, unexpected feelings taking hold. Attraction growing out of years of inseparable friendship. Holding hands giving way to a shocking first kiss, and the discovery and urgency that had soon followed. They'd started dating for real as sophomores. Then a late afternoon walk around the lake that fall had ended with the sweetest first time a boy growing into a man could have hoped for. And so he'd left his funny friend Jenn behind with his childhood, and had refused to call her anything but Jennifer since.

Used to drive Reverend Gardner crazy.

Now…

He couldn't deal with calling her *Jennifer*. Couldn't deal with her being here, so beautiful and sad and still, in the last place she was supposed to be—as if she'd been waiting for him all this time.

"I…" Pain crowded out the shock on her face. Her mouth opened and closed, but no other sound emerged.

"Jenn?" The irritating form of her name shielded him. Pissed him off. "What—"

"I…I stopped by to see if I could help—"

"Nitpick is more like it," a craggy voice grumped from behind her. Unsteady footsteps shuffled toward the door. "Years of no one giving a damn what goes on in this house, now it's like a parade traipsing through here."

Neal braced himself, locking onto Jenn's stare to keep his feet planted on the porch, instead of beating a path back to his car. Dread was too tame a word for the half-anxious, half-nauseous queasiness flooding his system as the door was yanked from her grasp and flung wide.

"Who the—" His father's tirade froze in midsentence when he caught sight of Neal.

Neal couldn't believe the man standing in front of him was his father. Unkempt beard, bloodshot eyes. The wasted pallor of someone who'd been bingeing on whatever vice drove him to not giving a shit the fastest.

"You son of a bitch," his father spat out. Then the man squinted an accusing glare at the stunned woman wringing her hands between them. "You little—"

"Jenn has nothing to do with me being here." It made no sense that Nathan would think she had, but rushing to Jenn's defense was as instinctive as breathing in the impossibly fresh scent of her hair, taking her essence into his lungs when what he craved was to have her back in his empty arms.

He reached toward her, wondering if some truly lost part of his mind had conjured her up. When she edged out of his grasp, he yanked his hand back, disgusted with himself.

Get a grip! You're scaring her to death.

"I had no idea Jenn still lived in Rivermist," he said. *Keep looking at the old man.* "Let alone that she'd be… Exactly what is she doing here?"

"Driving me crazy, with all her harping, that's what she's doing. You here to take a crack at what's left?"

Jenn's shoulders straightened as she built up steam to respond. Neal braced himself for another blast of her sweet voice. He finally looked her way again, forcing down his need for her. Forcing his "nothing gets in" expression to stay put.

Her eyes filled with tears, striking him even harder than her voice had. She shoved her hands into the pockets of well-worn, lovingly fitted jeans, stared at the ground for a beat, then glanced back up with a broken smile.

God, that smile.

"I should be going," she said as she escaped back down the shadowy hallway, toward the kitchen he'd once eaten in every morning. Her absence made it both possible and painful to breathe again.

"You got somethin' to say?" his father demanded. "'Cause I've had just about enough of—"

"Buford called me." Neal refocused on his one and only reason for being there. "You look like hell, and the man's worried."

Why bother with pleasantries? Whatever this moment was going to be, he'd known a warm reunion wasn't on the menu.

"You volunteering to babysit, too?" His father straightened to his full height for the first time, a good inch taller than Neal. He raised a shaking hand to push at the slimy hair falling into his eyes. The man smelled like a three-day binge. "You ready to give me your version of how much I got to live for?"

Nathan braced a shoulder on the doorjamb and winced against what looked like a whopper of a hangover.

Or was it?

How much I got to live for...

Neal looked to where Jenn had disappeared. Replayed the disjointed conversation spoken around him in the last few minutes.

She had been helping his father out around the house, but from the looks of the dust and cobwebs coating everything in sight, not for terribly long. And clearly not by invitation. At the same time that the man's condition had sent Buford reaching out long-distance to Neal.

Holy hell.

Neal stared at his father in denial. The man just stood there, waiting for him to catch a clue or get out. It didn't seem to matter which.

"You're dying?" It was an impossible thought.

"Like you care."

"Care!" Neal desperately needed to be in his Mustang—the one he'd bought and painstakingly restored because it was his father's favorite model—and speeding back down the road to Atlanta.

Except he couldn't move.

Jenn brushed against him as she hustled by, her head down. Her coat lay carelessly across one arm, despite the afternoon temperature that barely clung to the freezing mark. "I...I'll come back tomorrow, Nathan, to finish up the kitchen."

Neal watched her until she was out of sight. Biting his tongue barely stifled the urge to call her back. To not leave him alone with the reality waiting for him when he turned around.

His father was dying.

Slam!

And the bastard had just hit him in the ass with the front door.

HE ISN'T HERE.

Neal isn't really back.

Right, he wasn't back. And she hadn't just left through the front door, instead of the kitchen where she'd gone to get her coat, just to have an excuse to be near him one more time. To touch him before he disappeared again, like some ghost who'd waited for her most vulnerable moment since returning to Rivermist to mess with her head.

"Jenn!"

Her ghost was jogging toward her across the scarred front lawn, the effortless athletic grace of each stride stalling her just long enough for him to catch up. She turned her back, but there was no escape even in that. Parked behind her car was a shiny red Mustang, the make and model of the beautifully restored classic one hundred percent the Neal Cain she'd loved, no matter how the man behind her resembled a total stranger now.

"Jenn?"

His touch on her elbow was so light, maybe she'd imagined it. Imagined him coming after her like a weak confused part of her had wanted him to. But there was no ignoring the pressure he exerted as he turned her around.

"I'm sorry, I don't want to bother you… But, I—I need to know what's going on with Nathan."

Bother her?

Now why would him being here, making her feel things that would only destroy her again if she let them, bother her?

"Jenn?"

"I have to go." She fumbled for the door handle, shattered by him calling her anything but Jennifer. By the sound of him calling his father *Nathan*. There was nothing familiar in that tight voice. Deadness, instead of warmth, filled those eyes. So why did she want to crawl into his arms and cling to the reality of simply having him here, no matter how little of the boy she'd loved had returned in the body of this dangerous-looking man?

"Don't leave, please." Something in that calm expression shifted. A softening as he reached to thumb a tear from her cheek, only to stiffen before he actually touched her. "I know I'm upsetting you, but I need to know what's going on with Na—"

"You're going to have to talk with your father yourself." Finally managing to open the car door, she crawled inside. She had to get out of there, before she curled into a ball and burst into tears. "I'm sure you two have a lot to catch up on."

"He shut the door in my face." Neal held fast to the door frame, a fine tremor shaking his fingers.

"Mine, too." His distress worked its way through her panic. She forced herself to remember what this man's return could mean for Nathan, regardless of the disaster it already was for her. "But I got in. You will, too, Neal. I don't think your dad wants to be alone nearly as much as he pretends he does."

"He locked me out, Jenn."

"Then break the door down." She fired the engine, prepared to leave whether he let go or not.

Please let go.

But as he finally stepped back, the loss that had destroyed her in the courtroom years ago threatened to consume her all over again.

"Is EVERYTHING ALL RIGHT?" her dad called as Jenn and Mandy hurried in the front door, bringing the cold night in with them.

It was hours past the two o'clock she'd promised to return by.

"I'm sorry we're so late. I didn't make it back to pick up Mandy until after six. I'll get started on dinner."

"Dinner's fine. I popped a frozen pizza in the oven a few minutes ago. What happened at Nathan's? I was worried."

"Mandy, honey. Why don't you play upstairs for a bit until the pizza's ready?" Jenn forced a smile as she grabbed the coat off her twirling child. An everyday routine they followed without thinking, only today the normalcy of it earned Mandy an extra hug.

This child was a reminder of all Jenn had done right since leaving Rivermist in shame. Everything she could still do right in her life, if she stayed and kept trying, instead of running—which was exactly what she'd talked herself out of doing as she drove in circles for hours before finally driving to Ashley's.

"'Kay, Mommy." The six-year-old headed up the stairs, giving her grandfather plenty of space.

Disappointment flickered across his features.

"She'll get over this morning, Dad." Jenn patted his shoulder, then shucked off her own coat. "She loves you to pieces."

She found herself drowning in his gaze, the word *love* swirling in the perpetually choppy waters between them. If only she could claim for herself what she just had for her daughter—that she loved this man to pieces. But that kind of trust was beyond them still, just when she desperately needed it back.

Yet, he'd been worried about her, even if his concern came in the guise of heating an oven-baked pizza. That was something at least.

"Something's wrong," he said. "Is it Nathan?"

Nathan, Traci, Neal—where did she start?

Neal.

Her mind had refused to settle on anything else, no matter how pointless and painful it was to replay how tall and breathtakingly handsome he still was. He'd been right there in front of her. Touching her and talking to her. And she'd—

Stop it!

"Mr. Cain…" she began, forcing her thoughts back to what she dealt with best: other people's problems. "He's dying, Dad. Nathan Cain's dying."

"TELL ME YOU DIDN'T KNOW," Neal demanded as he barged past Buford's sputtering secretary and into the lawyer's office.

"Mr. Richmond?" asked the young girl manning what used to be Gretchen McCrady's desk.

"It's okay, Belinda." Buford waved her away and waited for the door to close before addressing Neal. "I take it you've seen your daddy's place for yourself. It's a shame how he's let that house go. I tried to tell you—"

"Screw the house." Neal dropped into the age-worn club chair that had been across from the man's desk since Buford and Nathan started the firm twenty-five years ago. "Tell me you didn't call me down here on the pretence of making sure my father saw a doctor, knowing full well the man was dying."

"Dying?" The leather of Buford's chair groaned as he leaned forward. "Who told you that?"

"Nathan! Sort of. The two of them were acting weird, then something he said hit me—only a minute before the front door did, when he locked me out. I've tried for hours to get him to open back up, but—"

"They?" Buford roused himself from his shock to zero in on the one part of Neal's ramblings he wanted to discuss the least. "Are you telling me your daddy had company?"

Neal pushed out of the chair and prowled to the opposite end of the office.

"Jenn Gardner was there."

Buford's low whistle ended in the man contemplating the hands he'd folded in his lap. "Now, ain't that somethin'. That girl and her family haven't said boo to the old goat since…well, since Nathan lost you, and Reverend and Mrs. Gardner lost Jenn. She must have known something was wrong, for her to—"

"What do you mean, the Gardners lost Jenn?" Neal had to sit down again.

She'd looked fine. Startled. Sad, presumably about Nathan. Blond and sweet and heart-stoppingly beautiful. And fine. He'd never expected happily ever after for her, but anything less than fine was unacceptable.

The hardened gaze of a tough-as-nails Southern lawyer assessed him. "You really have cut yourself off from this place, haven't you? You never wanted to catch up on local comings and goings when we talked investments and stock dividends. But I always figured you were getting the high points from somewhere. You have investigators, don't you, for those clients of yours? You mean to tell me you got no idea what happened to that girl after they carted you upstate?"

"I didn't even know she was still living here." Digging into Jenn's life would have meant caring about her again, and that would have been unbearable.

She'd been shooting for med school. If that hadn't worked out for her, there were other careers. Marriage. Kids. Whatever. Anything was better than the nightmare of him hunting her down after his parole would have been.

What the hell was going on?

"She told you your daddy was dying?" Buford's

question quivered with the same disbelief that still raged through Neal.

"No. She just stood there staring at the two of us, like she wanted to run and hide."

"Understandable." Buford nodded. "Considering…"

"Considering what?" *Damn it!* "Don't answer that. It's none of my business."

Chicken-shit.

Neal braced his elbows on his knees. "Just tell me what's wrong with my father and what he needs, so I can make it happen and get out of the man's way."

"Out of his way? You said Nathan's dyin—"

"And he doesn't want me here any more now than before he got sick with whatever's ailing him."

His father's reaction to seeing him again had said it all. And it had hurt, when nothing in Neal's world had hurt in a long time.

The room filled with the sound of the clock ticking in the corner. Nothing else moved.

"You're both full of it." Buford inhaled deeply. "That man's been waiting for you to show up for years. He—"

"Doesn't want a thing from me." And forcing Nathan to say it again wasn't going to solve anything. It certainly wasn't going to fabricate an eleventh-hour relationship out of years of nothing.

"What if your daddy needs you to stay, whether he wants you to or not?" Buford asked.

"That's not going to happen," he said. "I don't belong here in the middle of what he's going through," he said. "Good or bad, this is what he wants. How we both dealt with what happened. All I can do for him now is make sure he has the best medical care available and stay out of his hair. If Jenn's helping him, then I'm grateful." Whatever was going on between them looked more adversarial than nurturing, but that ranked right up there with everything else he should be keeping his nose out of. "If you can't tell me anything, I'll see his doctor before I head back out of town. I'll make whatever medical arrangements you think I legally can, and stay in touch from Atlanta. But I can't…"

"Hold Nathan's hand and watch him die?" The lawyer achieved both fury and sympathy in the same frown.

"God, Buford." Pressing his fingers against his closed eyelids, Neal tried to rub away the image of his father's pale complexion. The tremor of weakness in his hands, in his angry defiance. "Don't sugarcoat things on my account."

The ache in his chest burned higher.

"This is your chance to settle things, son. Don't turn your back on this place again. I don't care what that old goat said. Your daddy's life has become a shrine to giving up. Don't make the same mistake and run away again."

"I'm not running." It wasn't lost on Neal that he'd spent several hours that morning loitering on the outskirts of town contemplating doing just that. "I'm giving my father the distance he wants."

"Then I reckon it's a blessing the man's stumbled into Jenn Gardner's help." The lawyer sounded dubious.

"I guess so." Neal clenched his fists against the thought of his father's *blessing*, and what the woman had somehow managed to make him feel just by standing in front of him. She couldn't have sprinted away any faster, and all he'd wanted to do was reach out and hold on, until something—anything—made sense. He headed for the door. "I'm going to see what I can pry out of Doc Harden."

"Say, Neal…"

Shoulders sunk, he paused with the door half open. "What?"

"Take it easy on Jenn if you see her again." It wasn't a friendly request. "It blew most everyone's minds, her coming back here in the first place, after everything she's been through. Whether you want to know the details or not, that girl deserves a break. I got no idea where she found the nerve to approach Nathan the way you say she has, but I don't figure Reverend Gardner's too happy about it. Don't go and become part of her troubles again."

Neal jerked the door open and stomped through the waiting room he and Jenn had once played board games in—passing the time during rainy summer days. Mrs. McCrady had kept the games in the bottom drawer of her beaten-up desk.

Don't be part of Jenn's troubles? If trouble still haunted the woman, there was no doubt he already had his share of the blame, same as he did with his father. How could he not? He reached the street, then stalled, the outside air condensing around his face as he exhaled. The invisible coming to life before his eyes.

You don't want to leave, man. Admit it!

The worst of it was, he hadn't wanted his father to leave that last day they'd argued in prison, either. But he'd forced himself to let the man go. It had been the right thing then, same as leaving Nathan and Jenn in peace was the right thing now.

Only he couldn't stop remembering how he and his father had consoled each other after his mother's death, learning to love deeper to make up for her loss. His arms wouldn't stop aching for all the times he hadn't been there to hold Jenn, whatever she'd been through. He knew just how she liked to be cuddled, how perfectly her head fit on his shoulder. The magic of loving her. Of becoming a part of her with an honesty and completeness he hadn't been able to capture with any woman since his parole.

Churning, rolling up from the deepest part of him, the compulsion to do whatever he could for these people besides leaving again wouldn't let him go.

He'd thought staying away was the best he could do for the people he'd hurt here. Maybe he'd been wrong.

Maybe.

CHAPTER SEVEN

BANANAS. JENN NEEDED BANANAS. The fiber and the vitamins would be great for Nathan. Anything that dipped below the seventy-five-percent preservative threshold would be a slam dunk. She pushed her cart toward to the other side of the store.

Her quick stop at the Buy Right after church to replenish the dry goods she'd raided from her father's pantry, and to buy more essentials for Nathan Cain, was taking forever.

Forever was exactly how long she needed before she was ready to face the Cain house again.

Had Neal gotten in to see his father? Would he be there today?

So what if he was? She'd simply leave the men to it, same as yesterday, and be grateful Nathan was no longer alone. That the two of them had this time to make things between them right.

Neal was back in Rivermist for his father, not her. He couldn't have made that more clear. There would be no more heartbreakingly awkward conversations between the two of them, thank God. No more silent moments of staring at what she'd never have again. Too much had happened between them for there to be anything but silence now. She'd make this one last gesture, bring Nathan one last care package, then bow out as gracefully as possible after her mad dash to her car yesterday afternoon.

Assuming Neal was there at all.

After church that morning, her dad had offered to watch Mandy for the rest of the day. That left Jenn plenty of time to take care of the dying old friend he was clearly concerned about. *If Neal can't help the man, I'm glad...I'm glad Nathan has you,* her dad had said last night. It had blown her away. Witnessing genuine concern for a man he hadn't spoken to for the better part of a decade had been like glimpsing a tiny bit of yesterday. And he hadn't even pressured her for a reaction to seeing Neal again, beyond a softly spoken, "Are you okay?"

She took a blind turn around a display of Fruit-O's, hit the home stretch to produce, and—wham!—ran right into the back of a man reading something from the magazine rack.

"I'm so sorry." She hurried to his side. When he turned to face her, she stumbled back. "Jeremy!"

It was creepy, the way Bobby Compton's younger brother kept turning up, conveniently in her path and never exactly surprised to see her. He was home from whatever college he was pursuing an MBA at—taking a semester off before he graduated, she'd heard his mother complain at the dry cleaners. He'd just shown up several weeks ago, unannounced, and had refused to reenroll until the spring.

"Are you okay?" he asked.

She nodded.

Sure. Gaping at a ringer for his dead brother was a piece of cake.

"Shouldn't I be asking you that?" She moved the cart another inch away from his butt.

"No problem." He grinned good-naturedly.

The guy was only a few years her junior, but he would forever be the obnoxious pest who'd tagged along when they were kids, whenever Neal and Bobby would let him. And his increasingly attentive interest when most people—including his mother—made a point of avoiding her, wasn't helping his pest quotient.

He glanced behind her. "Where's the kid?"

Jenn's spine stiffened. She quietly suffered every slanted look and public snubbing Jeremy's mother dished out. To Mrs. Compton, she and Neal would forever be the murderers who'd never pay enough for taking her baby away from her, and the woman was entitled to her say. Jeremy, on the other hand, could take a flying leap. Particularly today.

"She's with her grandfather," Jenn managed

calmly. Friendly would have invited more conversation.

"Oh, right." His expression heated from total lack of interest to that come-on leer she no longer thought she was imagining. "You always look so great."

She jumped at the feel of his palm on her arm. A cold sweat broke out between her shoulder blades. She'd been nice but distant each time they'd talked, hoping he'd catch the hint. She worried about his feelings more than she would any other creepy guy, because she was part of the reason his mother seemed unable to approve of Jeremy, because he'd never be as perfect as his dead, older brother.

She tried easing away now, but his grip tightened. She insisted, yanking until he turned her loose. It had been a long time since she'd invited a man's touch. Any man but Neal, whom she'd had the insane urge to launch herself at not more than a second after seeing him again yesterday.

"Just as pretty as ever." Jeremy's smile dipped closer to creepy this time. "Man, we had some good times, didn't we?"

After Bobby's death, his mother had become Rivermist's moral authority. But that hadn't stopped Jeremy from leading the fast and loose crowd Jenn fell in with after Neal's conviction. Her part in his family's loss had almost seemed to heighten his interest in a way that she'd known was wrong even then.

"Things have changed." She took another step away. "Besides, I've had enough good times to last me for a while."

"I was over at Bandit's lounge the other day." Irritation seeped through the invitation in his voice. "They've got a ton of Springsteen on the jukebox. Whataya say we check it out tonight? Could be fun."

Springsteen and Jeremy, and enough weed and vodka to guarantee she couldn't think straight.

Yeah, those were the good ol' days.

"I have to go," she said. "I have a really busy day."

"I hear you were over at old Mr. Cain's place yesterday. That Neal is back." His hand stalled the cart she was inching backward, his eyes hardening as they looked over her shoulder toward the automatic doors at the entrance. "I bet you'd make time fast enough if that son of a bitch came sniffing around for a date."

Which meant what, exactly? That Jeremy was pissed he hadn't managed to get a fresh piece of her first. It was a bizarre thought, but—

"Long time no see, man," he sneered, his attention trained on whoever was behind her.

Jenn flinched at the sound of approaching footsteps, her heart fluttering in her chest at the insane hope that Neal would be there when she turned around. When she spun to find him several feet away, her heart seemed to give up beating altogether.

No matter that she'd convinced herself they wouldn't see each other again. She'd dreamed of him last night, anyway. Of them. Of a lifetime ago, and what their lives might have been like if so much hadn't happened.

"Jeremy." Neal's attention dropped to where the other man held her cart in a viselike grip.

Survival instincts taking hold, she made good on her escape. She felt their stares follow her all the way to the produce section, but she refused to look back. Refused to hope it was Neal following her when she heard someone approaching.

"Jenn." His touch was soft on her elbow; the name he used a harsh reminder that this was no dream. "Can we talk for a minute? It's about Nathan."

"Nathan?" She couldn't help but turn. "Since when do you call him anything but *Dad?*"

Neal only stared in response. He still looked the part of a hard-as-nails businessman, even if his suit was slightly more wrinkled this morning. Too-dark, too-calm eyes studied her from a face that showed no hint of the jumbled mess of loss and hope and regret that had been churning inside her since yesterday.

"Did you two finally talk?" It hurt to look at him, so she began cataloguing the contents of her cart.

"I wouldn't be here, putting you through this, if we had." The rasp of his voice made her wonder if he'd slept any better than she had last night. "I need to know how long you've been helping him."

"I...I only came over for the first time yesterday." She was twirling her hair, she realized, and he was watching her. Making her wish he'd reach out and run his hands through it, the way he once would have. Exactly the kind of pointless wishing that made talking with him like this a really bad idea. "It didn't take long to see that your dad wasn't well, that his crankiness is more bark than bite."

Without warning, the corner of Neal's mouth lifted into a smile. "You always were a soft touch."

"He's been trying to kill himself for years," she bit out. If she sounded angry, it was only at herself. There was no place for that smile in her world now, a fun fact that it shouldn't be so hard to keep in mind. She cleared her throat before continuing. "It didn't take a soft touch to see that and want to help him."

"But why you?" The smile was gone. A hard look replaced it. Neal would have no way of knowing that she'd seen exactly the same expression on his father's face yesterday, or what the similarity between the two men was doing to her determination to keep her distance.

"What?" She'd completely lost track of his question.

"Why you? From what Buford's told me, the man's done everything he can to run the rest of the town off. Why did he open the door for you? What's your secret?"

He no longer sounded so detached from the situation. In fact, he sounded just the tiniest bit jealous. Her resistance softened.

"I wouldn't let him drive me away. I wouldn't let him keep thinking I didn't care about him." It was what she wanted for Neal, too. For him and Nathan both. They still had some time, if Neal would only give it a chance.

"He's locked me out." Neal shook his head. "And I—"

"He'll change his mind eventually. Keep trying."

"No. He won't, and I—"

"Neal—" She reached for his arm, refusing to believe that the amazing young man who'd felt too much responsibility to avoid paying for his friend's death could give up this easily on his own father.

"I need your help, Jenn." He evaded her touch. "That's why I stopped when I saw your car outside. I have no right to ask for anything after all this time, but I don't know where else to turn. Are you going to keep seeing him? Are you going back over there today?"

Neal needed her.

"Yes, but—

"Then will you keep in touch with me about his condition? I'm heading back to Atlanta, and—"

"Heading back?" The stupidity of what he'd said kicked her temper into gear. "You haven't been in town for twenty-four hours, and you're leaving again?"

"There's nothing for me to do here but cause trouble." His beautiful eyes dimmed with the kind of regret that couldn't not affect her. "I was awake all night at the hotel, trying to get my mind around this. There's nothing else to do."

She was tempted to thunk him upside the head for being so dense. "How about trying to get through to him again? That would be a good start."

"I did after you left yesterday!" He ran a hand through his hair. "I did everything but shatter a window to get back into that falling-down old place. The man ignored me. What else am I supposed to do if my father wants me out of here that badly, but let him die in peace?"

He practically shouted his last question. He was close to coming unglued. A sight most people in Rivermist might have backed away from, given Neal's prison stint and the sheer size and muscle he'd put on since anyone here had last seen him. But Jenn could never be afraid of him, no matter how much of a stranger he'd become. And she, of all people, understood what it had cost him to come back to Rivermist. How badly he still needed to leave this place behind.

"You try again." She stepped closer, rather than

away. "And then again, for as long as it takes. It'll be worth it, when your dad finally trusts you enough to let you in. Once he remembers that you're still a family, even after everything that's happened."

"Even if that were possible—" Neal's head was shaking "—I can't stay. I have an important case back in Atlanta. Clients I can't bail on."

"Clients?" she asked, then she remembered. "The word around town is that you're a lawyer now, like your dad."

His expression hardened.

"Convicted felons aren't allowed to practice law, Jenn."

The word *felon* slapped her hard.

She refused to see him that way. She always had.

"So if you're not a lawyer, then you..."

"I help society's castoffs maneuver Atlanta's over-taxed, understaffed legal system, and I make sure they get a fair shot. I had a lot of time on my hands in prison. There was the gym, the gangs or the library. I chose the books. Reading kept me from howling at the moon, so I devoured everything I could get my hands on. Every law book they had."

Of course he'd chosen books. And his father's favorite books at that. He'd scored a 1530 on his SATs. Colleges had been heavily recruiting him, for both academics and football. There was a time when he'd had the world by the tail.

They both had.

"I'm taking night courses at Georgia State Law School whenever I have the chance," he continued, falling into the easy rhythm of conversation that was second nature to people who'd known each other all their lives. Except, Jenn reminded herself, they didn't know each other at all anymore.

"But, you said you couldn't—"

"Practice law in a courtroom?" He waved away the thought. "That's just going through the motions. The real work is done on the outside. Most cases never make it before a jury. Once they reach a court-room, the verdict's usually in the bag—either through plea bargains or pretrial briefs and confer-ences with a judge. I offer free legal aid. My defend-ants can't afford their own attorneys, and I make sure they don't get lost in the system."

"You're helping people who have nowhere else to turn." Pride for what he'd become warmed her. "If you can do that after everything you've been through, I know you can get through to your dad. You just have to keep trying. He needs you, Neal. More than either one of you realizes."

"Come on, Jenn." The deadness in his voice was that of a man still in prison—only this one, of his own making. "You and I both know that me staying here is the last thing anyone in Rivermist needs."

He held out a business card.

"Will you call me?" he asked casually, as if she hadn't ached to do just that for years after he'd left. "Let me know if Nathan needs anything? If there's any…any change in his condition that I should know about?"

Looking from him to the cart full of healthy food she was buying for a man who wasn't going to get better no matter what he ate, she chastised the weak place inside her that wanted to jump at the excuse to hear Neal's voice again.

It would be better for her if he left, if he went back to where he'd come from and away from her need for more and more of him, until she destroyed herself wanting him again. Neal being anywhere near her life now was a mistake—a life he hadn't wanted to know anything about since they were kids.

But Nathan Cain needed his son back.

"I'm sorry." She made herself turn away. "I can't do that. Not if it's going to make it easier for you to leave."

I'M AT THE GAS STATION around the corner from my house, Traci had said over the phone during Monday night's dinner. *I need to talk.*

Five minutes later, Jenn was on the road to meet her.

The girl's appointment at the clinic had been that morning. Her teeth had been chattering, and not just from the night's cold. Obviously the news from the doctor, and the day Traci had had to deal with the ramifications, had finally convinced her she didn't want to go through this alone.

At least Jenn hoped so.

Her dad had agreed to finish helping Mandy with her homework. Things had shifted more than a little between them. He still hadn't offered to help outright, still hadn't visited Nathan himself, but he'd stopped discouraging her from going back to the Cain place. So she'd spent yesterday disinfecting the rest of the man's kitchen and trying not to be discouraged that Neal hadn't shown up. Today, while Mandy was in school, had been another whirlwind of endless projects around Nathan's place. And still no Neal.

Her dad had been hard at work himself, pumping the rumor mill. Neal was still paying for a room at the town's only hotel, the story was, but he and his vintage car had been seen speeding out of town yesterday afternoon. News she'd rather not have known, but the fact that her father had gone out of his way to find out for her had meant the world.

He was working harder at seeing her as an adult. Seemed committed to keeping her in Rivermist this time. If he only knew what she was keeping from him as she rushed to see Traci Carpenter, he might just change his mind.

She reached the Stop and Pump in record time. Like most businesses in Rivermist, the station closed at seven on weeknights. But security lights lent the parking lot plenty of artificial light. She braked her ten-year-old car beside Traci's spanking new one.

The teenager stared at Jenn from behind the wheel. Finally, she stepped out, dread slowing her approach. Her black jeans and a sparkly, low-cut red top said "Night on the Town," but her artfully applied makeup was smudged and tracked with tears. Hair that was usually styled to perfection had been roughly shoved into a ponytail. The teenager that sat beside Jenn and slammed the door looked like a little girl doing a lousy job of playing dress-up.

Jenn took her hand. "You're freezing."

"I've been driving around for hours." The teen's dazed voice was as unfocused as her eyes.

Jenn flipped her heater to high. "Is this about your appointment this morning?"

Traci flinched. "I...I couldn't go home after school. I...I went to see..." She pulled away and hugged herself protectively.

"You went to see your guy, didn't you? Does he—"

"I'm not telling you where he lives. Don't even try to get me to."

Teenagers could look so tough when they were terrified.

"I don't care about anything but you right now. What did the clinic's tests say?"

Those tough eyes watered. Traci bit her lip, as if not saying the words would make the truth go away.

"So you *are* pregnant," Jenn said, keeping the conversation flowing, years of training and practical application kicking in.

"Yeah." Traci dropped her head.

"And your guy?" The next few steps were so important. The rest of the teen's life would be shaped by the choices she made over the next weeks and months. "You told him, right?"

Traci's laugh wasn't the answer Jenn had hoped for.

"You were right." The girl's hand muffled her watery words. "I mean, I'm not stupid. I knew he wasn't going to be thrilled with the idea of having a baby. But I thought he loved me. I thought he'd at least take care of me, that he'd try and make things better."

"What did he say?" Jenn sucked down the urge to pay this loser boyfriend a visit and make sure he was suffering as much as the young woman sitting beside her.

"He didn't have to say anything." Traci turned her face completely toward Jenn for the first time.

Okay. Suffering wasn't good enough for the jackass.

"Oh, honey." Traci's swollen right eye was already turning a nasty shade of magenta.

"He threw me out of his apartment. He's done with me. S-said never t-to call him again."

Jenn tipped the girl's face to get a better look and winced. "We need to get this checked out at the hospital."

"And broadcast it to everyone in town?"

"Everyone's going to know in the morning. You can't hide this."

"I'll tell everyone at school I fell."

"What about your parents? They need to know what happened. They'll want a doctor to see you, even if you don't tell them about the baby. And a doctor will—"

"I can't!"

"Can't see your parents?" Treading carefully, Jenn curled her hands around the steering wheel. "Or can't tell them about the baby?"

"Both."

"Traci—"

"No, I don't want anyone else to know."

"You'll need to see a doctor eventually. And you'll want your mom there, trust me."

Jenn would have given anything to have had her mother's shoulder to lean on during each lonely, terrifying prenatal visit.

Traci's mouth gaped. "You're kidding, right? My mother, the world's best Girl Scout leader, best PTA president, best bake sale coordinator, holding my hand while I have an abortion?"

"Abortion!" Jenn's ears buzzed.

At every shelter she'd worked in since college, she'd asked to work with runaways, teen mothers, battered women. She'd never trusted herself to remain objective and impartial during abortion counseling. She'd come too close to that decision herself. And every day with Mandy was a reminder of the blessing she'd almost thrown away. The precious life that almost wasn't. But there was no way she would force her convictions on another young woman's right to make her own choice.

"You...you're not ready to make that kind of decision yet," she hedged.

"I can't have this baby! My parents would kill me if they found out."

Jenn recalled the sight of Bob Carpenter slipping his arm around his wife's shoulders the last time the couple had visited her dad. Betty punching him affectionately. They'd been teasing each other about their never-ending redecorating plans.

There was a lot of love there. Too much love to give up on without even trying.

"They'll be upset, Traci. But in the end, I think they'll support whatever you decide to do."

"Yeah?" The teenager's sneer had fangs. "Just like your parents supported you, right?"

Touché.

"It's too soon to be making any decisions," she repeated. "You're upset, and you need to give this some time. Hear all the facts at least before you act."

"I don't need facts." Traci's voice thinned to a whine. "I just want this to be over."

"The doctor won't give you a choice, Traci. Counseling is required before a pregnancy is terminated, and there's usually at least a twenty-four-hour waiting period before they'll perform the procedure. Young girls in your situation are advised to wait a few weeks."

"Why? So you and my parents can talk me into changing my mind!"

"You can bet I'm not going to let you do anything on impulse." Jenn laid a hand on Traci's shoulder. "I care about you, and I don't want you to make a hasty decision you might regret for the rest of your life."

"My only regret would be keeping this baby." Traci shrugged Jenn's hand off. "Its father doesn't care about me, and there's no way I can raise it by myself. And don't tell me how understanding my parents will be. Look at what yours did. Look at what keeping your baby did to your life."

Jenn had always talked frankly with her kids about the mistakes she'd made. About their consequences. The decision to keep this pregnancy or not was one of the most important decisions Traci would ever make. And thankfully, she was allowing Jenn to be a part of it. Which meant Jenn would calmly absorb whatever verbal crap the girl threw at her, then she'd return each argument with a promise that there was still hope. That she'd be there, waiting, until the girl was ready to hear something besides her own fear and panic.

"What happened to my life," she said quietly, "happened because of me and the choices I made. My life fell apart because I was doing everything I could to destroy it. Not because I had Mandy. And not because of my parents."

"Yeah, well, I wasn't trying to destroy anything." Traci wiped her nose with her sleeve. "I was in love. And now I'm alone. I want this to be over with. Are you going to help me or not?"

Jenn leaned her head back. Stared out into the night. Situations with no win-win solutions were nothing new for her. Neither was doing damage control when a crisis blew out of nowhere and dumped her on her ass. But she'd been dumped a little too much the past few days, even for her. And maybe she was finally over being everyone's go-to girl. Over saying, *Yes, I'll take care of that*, when any other sane person would say no.

So what was she going to do, give up? Leave Traci to give up on the future she might have with her baby, because the girl seemed hell-bent on not listening even though she'd called Jenn for help?

I need to talk.

"Jenn?" Traci's timid voice filled the tiny car. The same scared little-girl voice as when she'd called. "Are you going to help me? I don't have anywhere else to go."

"Of course I'll help you."

Jenn curbed the impulse to turn the girl over to her parents. Made herself see past the problems her decision would cause not just for her, but her father, too. The little piece of now here in Rivermist that she'd wanted so badly for her and Mandy was imploding. The fragile bond of healing growing between her and her father, the joy she'd found working with the kids in the church group, it was all teetering on the brink. But she couldn't leave Traci to face what was ahead alone.

She knew what that kind of loneliness felt like. Had felt it again this weekend, both times she'd walked away from Neal and the crazy need still deep inside to grab back a speck of what she'd had only with him.

That kind of loneliness was devastating. Destructive. Life-destroying.

Tonight, and any other night Traci needed her until she figured out how to face her decisions on her own, Jenn would be exactly where she was now. Between this child and the future Jenn refused to let Traci give up on so easily.

CHAPTER EIGHT

"WHAT ARE YOU STILL doing up, Dad?" Jenn asked. The hall clock had chimed two-fifteen when she walked past, but the light had still been on in her father's bedroom and his door was open. There was no point putting this off till morning.

"Waiting for you." He was sitting in the recliner beside his bed, reading by lamplight. "You were so upset by that phone call. Do you want to talk about it?"

The sincerity of his offer should have been comforting. It made her squirm instead.

"I can't."

"But something's wrong?"

"Yes." *If you could call talking a desperate teen out of having a hasty abortion something wrong.*

He nodded in silence. It must have taken Herculean restraint not to press for more details, but, bless him, he didn't.

"I wish I could tell you more...." Or ask for advice. The need to not be in this alone was almost her undoing.

"Someone's in trouble, aren't they?" her father finally asked. "Someone besides Nathan?"

"Yes."

"One of your kids?"

She didn't even blink in response. She didn't dare.

"Someone in my congregation?" His voice tightened. "Someone I'm responsible for, and you're not going to tell me, is that it?"

"I can't, Dad. Not yet. I gave my word."

"I can only assume if it's important enough to keep you out this late, that you're making sure the child's parents are involved."

"I can't talk about that, either." She hated what she was doing at that moment, and how his expression shifted into disappointment.

Nothing Jenn said had changed Traci's mind. The teenager was determined to keep her pregnancy a secret. To deal with her parents by not dealing with them. Going to school tomorrow as if nothing had happened. But she'd agreed to meet up with Jenn again in the afternoon. That was something at least. Maybe a night of tossing and turning would convince the kid to involve her parents in her decision. Maybe this didn't have to end ugly for all of them.

"This person trusts me," Jenn said, holding tight to her promise. "I can't betray that."

"You have an obligation to the parents to let them know the child's in trouble. And you have a responsibility to the church leadership as well. To me. You made that commitment when you asked to work with the youth."

"My responsibility is to do what I think is right, regardless of where I work." And there it was, in big, bold letters.

The fundamental difference in their views of right and wrong. Her father's faith was in the institution of the church, hers was in her relationships with the kids in her care. Neither one of them was wrong, but that didn't mean they could work together to help someone like Traci.

"Someone who feels there's nowhere else to turn has turned to me," she said. "I can't betray that. If you can't respect my judgment in anything else, please trust that I'm doing everything I can for this child."

"I do respect your judgment, Jenn, whether you can find a way to believe me now or not." He shut his book and sat higher against the recliner's worn cushions. "Your mother and I made some terrible mistakes with you, and I can't begin to imagine what you went through. But you survived, and I couldn't be prouder. And somehow, through everything, you've learned how to be there for other people. To understand what they need and then make sure they get it. You've done an amazing job raising Mandy, even if I don't always agree with your methods.

She's wonderful. Both of you are. You've even gotten Nathan Cain to let you help him, and that's…that's nothing short of a miracle. But…"

He was proud of her. He was sorry. How long had she dreamed of him saying just that?

"But…" Jenn went in and sat on the edge of the bed, waiting, all too aware she was about to blow this place of understanding they'd finally achieved straight to hell.

Please, Dad. Don't let me hurt you again.

"But it occurs to me that you've also gotten really good at taking other people's problems on your shoulders, as if they were your own. It's like you can't walk away when someone asks for help, regardless of the cost."

You think?

Her manager at the clinic in Raleigh had noted her issues with overidentification on her last performance review. Inappropriate boundaries. The line of professional caregiver becoming blurred. Her clients' issues and setbacks becoming too personal.

All because, she'd realized, it was safer to deal with other people's needs than it was her own. But knowing the reason didn't make the impulse any easier to curb. Or the gratification of seeing the lives she worked with changed for the better any less addictive. The problem had been getting worse for years, instead of better. The indefinite leave she'd taken to move down here to be with her father had been considered best for all concerned.

"I can't not help when I know I can make a difference," she argued now, same as she had with her supervisor.

"Sacrificing your own well-being to help someone else?" her father asked. "Keeping a secret that shouldn't be kept? I don't see how that's helping anyone. The church's guidelines for working with the youth are clear—"

"I know."

"If you put me in a position where I can't be a pastor and support you as a father at the same time, I—"

"You'll be a pastor first, I know. And you should." She rubbed her eyes with the heels of her hands. "I know where your priorities have to be, Dad."

He put a hand on her knee. "Your emotions have led you into some destructive choices in the past, Jenn. Whatever's going on with this child, I'm sure you think you're doing the right thing. But—"

"I'll involve you as soon as I can." She couldn't hear another *but*. "And I guess we'll have to take it from there. You're right about my role at the church, though. I need to step away from working with the youth group before this situation gets out of hand."

"I, for one, would be sorry to see that happen." Her shock must have shown on her face. "Your approach has been an unqualified success. The size of your Saturday gatherings has doubled in just a couple of months. It's like the kids know they can trust you. Don's excited about how many have signed up for the ski trip you suggested. I was looking forward to working with you when I return full-time next month."

Don Holloway, the associate pastor and part-time youth minister who'd been holding down the fort while her father worked sporadic part-time hours during his recovery, had been Jenn's only genuine support at the church. Her resignation would only add to his burden.

And the hits just kept on coming.

"Everyone was right from the start about me not being a good fit." She'd known better, but she hadn't been able to walk away.

"I'm not as sure about that as I used to be." Her dad studied the worn carpet at his feet. "There's a lot I'm not really sure about anymore."

She couldn't stand it. Not another minute. He was supposed to be arguing with her. Protecting himself and his job. Playing it safe. She was off the bed before she had time to change her mind and hugging his neck. Squeezing even tighter when he brought his hands up to cup her shoulders. It couldn't last, but for just that moment, this man was laying aside his absolutes and seeing her as she really was, maybe even learning to accept her, disappointments and all.

"I think that's the nicest thing you've ever said to me, Dad."

And nice had never been harder to hear.

"YOU'RE PREGNANT, for real?" Shelly Ackerson asked Traci between second and third period.

Shelly was wearing her new sweater, the one she'd bought from the Abercrombie & Fitch catalogue she and Traci drooled over every chance they got.

Traci had told her because she'd needed someone besides Jenn Gardner to help her figure this out.

"Your mom must be having a cow!" Shelly was finding Traci's dilemma a bit too entertaining.

"It's my dad I'm worried about." Traci pulled her history book from her locker and slammed the door shut. Her friend did the same. "But I haven't told them yet."

"No wonder the local media hasn't been alerted."

Shelly blew a bubble with the gum school regs said she shouldn't be chewing. If you got caught smacking the stuff in the hallway, it was detention for a week.

God! The adults in this town cared about the stupidest things.

"This might be the one time in the history of mankind that Betty'll keep a lid on our family's dirty laundry," Traci added.

Surprisingly, her black eye and refusal last night to even open her mouth about where it had come from hadn't become instant gossip. Betty—the woman had stopped being Mom, right about the time Traci started seeing He-Who-Would-Never-Again-Be-Named— and Shelly's mom were best friends. But there had been no emergency phone call to the Ackerson house. No request to the community prayer chain for support and sympathy. It was as if her parents knew something worse was coming at their perfect world, and they didn't want to talk it about any more than Traci did.

"What does Carter—" Traci's stare stopped Shelly midsmack. "Sorry. What does *the jackass* want to do about it?"

"He wants it, and me, to go away for good." Traci rifled through her knapsack and pulled out her own chunk of contraband Hubba Bubba. She was really living on the edge these days. *Woo-hoo!* But chewing made her purple eye hurt even worse, so she stopped. Everything hurt worse this morning. "At least I think that's what his fist was trying to say when he threw it at me."

She rolled the fruity gum around with her tongue, hoping its sweetness would settle the swamp that used to be her stomach.

"So that's good, right?" Shelly asked.

Yeah, it was all good. Just another sunny day in Mayberry.

Traci headed to American history class, her best friend since preschool fast on her heels.

"I mean, now he can't cause any trouble, you know?" Shelly tucked her auburn, shoulder-length hair behind her ear and leaned closer. "Did Ms. Gardner say she'd help you with the...the thing?"

Her friend's question ended in a whisper, complete with a lame hand gesture that Traci figured was supposed to be the charades version of an abortion.

"No," she whispered back. "But she's keeping her mouth shut for now. You know, giving me a chance to decide what I'm going to—"

"Decide?" Shelly yanked her to a stop. "You're not thinking about keeping it!"

"*It* is a baby, Shelly!" Traci pulled away. What was it Jenn had said once, like months ago? That having Mandy had been the best thing that had happened in her life, no matter what it had cost her?

"How can I *not* think about keeping it?" Despite the show Traci put on for Bob and Betty's benefit, the pains she took to look as bored as the rest of her friends did with their parents, she hadn't ignored *everything* they'd tried to teach her. "How am I going to face my parents every day once I get rid of it?"

"It'll be a whole lot harder to face them with a drooling brat on your hip. Do what you have to do to salvage your life."

"Jeez, Shelly. You make it sound like I'm getting my nails done. We're talking about a baby."

Traci rushed past her friend and their history class. Before long, she was running. The sound of her footsteps bounced off the school's ugly green walls, clamoring in her head as her stomach swam.

What kind of moron picked green for school colors!

She flung the door open to the deserted bathroom and stumbled into a stall. Her black-and-white-checked backpack, the one her mother had special-ordered from a boutique in Atlanta, skidded across the filthy floor as she dropped to her knees and retched up the bagel she'd eaten for breakfast. When there was nothing left to hurl, but her stomach was still heaving, she groaned, wishing the bathroom—no, the entire school—would come crashing down and take her with it.

"God, what am I going to do?" The empty prayer bounced off the walls surrounding her, as if laughing at how lame it was to be looking for that kind of help now.

Why! *Why* hadn't she listened to her uptight parents? Why was *the jackass* the only person she'd listened to for months.

She'd been so cool. Too cool to care about who she hurt. Too cool to let anyone or anything rock her charmed life. Not her parents or Brett. And certainly not a baby.

Yeah, it was so cool to be puking her guts up three times a day. To have the only way she could get back to what was left of her life be killing her unborn baby. She leaned against the side of the stall, the sick taste coating her mouth threatening to make her even cooler still.

Saturday at Freddy's, she'd been so sure there was some easy fix. Some answer Jenn could magically produce to get her unpregnant and out of the jam she'd refused to believe she was in. She couldn't be pregnant, and most definitely not pregnant and alone. No boyfriend. No father for her child. No one else to make the decisions she didn't want to have to make.

Except what Jenn had done was tell her to face facts. To face up to her choices. Maybe even face her parents.

The woman was such a tool.

The facts were that towns like Rivermist held people's mistakes up for public viewing. The bigger the fall, the better the entertainment. Every indiscretion was milked for full shock value. What else was anyone going to do around here? Some people, like Jenn, never lived down their pasts.

But there the woman was, moving back home, loving her kid, facing down her disapproving father and his disapproving cronies. Making things better for Traci and the rest of the kids. Living her life, just to spite how convinced Traci was that hers was over. Even hooking up with that scary old guy, Mr. Cain, and helping him when no one else cared.

Jenn Gardner, the pariah, was a downright hero to most of the kids. Meanwhile Traci was hiding out like a loser, hugging a Rivermist High School toilet bowl because the woman's *help* had made it impossible for her to take the easy way out.

She grabbed her backpack, grimacing at the sight of her half-chewed gum stuck to its bottom. Digging inside the front pocket, she found the business card Jenn had insisted all the kids take at their first Teens in Action outing. Raleigh Teen and Prenatal Counseling Center, it read, followed only by Jenn's name and cell number. No pressure. No sales pitch. No, "You have to agree with me!"

God, why couldn't the woman have turned out to be the loser so many people thought she was?

Then maybe her simple, no-pressure advice wouldn't have wormed its way through Traci's freaked-out panic. And maybe Traci wouldn't be so desperate to do the unthinkable. To get the inevitable over with and see if, just maybe, there was a bit of a hero inside her, too.

Pulling out her cell phone, she started to cry as she pressed the numbers. She'd never, ever forgive the woman if this only made things worse.

"Mom?" she said when the cell connected, a

very uncool sob breaking free at the sound of her mother's concerned voice. "Mom, I'm coming home. I want…I need to talk."

"CAN I SPEAK WITH JENN, Reverend Gardner?" Neal asked in response to the minister's *Good Lord* after he'd opened the door.

Stephen Creighton had stared at Neal in exactly that same I-must-be-losing-it way when Neal called him into the office last night and told him he was taking an indefinite leave of absence to deal with his father. The lawyer's shock might have been over Neal having a father in the first place, but most likely it had been his announcement that he was making Stephen lead attorney on all their cases until further notice.

Keep me in the loop, send me briefs, e-mail me updates, but I need you to take charge. You did fine on the Martinez case last week. I trust you to deal with the rest.

As a rule, Neal never trusted anyone. But Stephen was summa cum laude from Emory Law, with a head full of too much book sense but better instincts than most seasoned attorneys. Instincts Neal was paying a fortune to temper the single-mindedness he wasn't completely unaware could interfere with his own objectivity from time to time. The man could more than handle the work solo for a while, and Neal had

finally accepted that for now he couldn't be anywhere *but* Rivermist.

"Reverend Gardner? I wouldn't ask if it wasn't
important. Is Jenn home?"

He'd spent all last night pouring over his investigator's report of the last eight years of Jenn's life,
and he almost wished he hadn't followed Buford's
offhand suggestion. He knew it all now. Had told
himself over and over that the truth didn't change
a thing. But somewhere during the night, seeing
her again, trying to understand what had happened,
had become just as important as getting through to
his father.

All these years, he'd made himself forget what it
was like to simply be there, next to her. He'd managed
to make himself forget how to feel altogether. But
each time he'd seen Jenn over the weekend, the
feelings and the memories had rushed back, as tena-
cious as they were unwelcome. As was his feeling of
responsibility for what she'd been through.

He'd been a part of the catastrophe that had destroyed her life. He didn't know how to make up for
that, how to make any of it better for her now. But
he'd be damned if he wasn't going to try.

"She's over with your daddy, I believe," the
aging man before him said. "I'd invite you in to
wait, but—"

"I understand." Neal straightened the silk tie he'd

worn with his best suit for one last meeting in the office that morning. He purposely hadn't changed clothes before driving out, despite his determination not to care what this man or anyone else in town thought of him now. "I know me being here can only cause problems for you. I was just hoping—"

"That's not what I meant." Reverend Gardner did some fidgeting with his own clothes. "It's just that maybe if you met up with Jenn at your father's, then…well, maybe you'd have better luck with Nathan this time."

Neal's investigator had gathered plenty of information on Nathan, too. On this entire town.

"How's your luck been with my father lately?" He didn't miss the tremor in the other man's hand as the reverend stopped smoothing his cardigan. "Or is your daughter still the only one around here who's managed to work up the interest to visit him?"

"I'm the last person your father wants to see, Neal." There was genuine regret in the admission.

"I seriously doubt that, sir," Neal said, turning away. "Somehow, I seriously doubt it."

Neal, is your father going to be okay? Stephen had asked as Neal left that morning.

No, he's dying, had been his simple response as he'd come to grips with coming back and seeing both Nathan and Jenn again. *He's dying, and he doesn't think I give a damn.*

"YOU GOT A BURR up your butt, or are you finally wising up and wanting the heck out of here?" Nathan Cain put more muscle behind the scraper and shaved off another chunk of dead paint and rotten windowsill.

The shutters that looked like crumbling skeletons were next. Like it mattered what the house he was going to croak in looked like.

"Neither. It's nothing." Jenn, all bundled up in her coat, raked more debris from under Wanda's azaleas. Her motions were as jerky and brittle as her fake smile.

She hadn't asked about Neal once since his boy's drive-by visit, which suited Nathan just fine. Turning his son away and not knowing if he'd ever see the kid again had been one of the hardest damn things he'd ever done. Didn't seem to be wearing on the girl much easier.

She'd maneuvered him outside to tackle the yard before he'd known what hit him—simply by picking up that damned rake herself and not caring if he followed or not. Some ridiculous throwback to the gentleman inside him had refused to sit and watch while she broke her back working on his place. So he'd joined her—after she'd cooked him lunch and then watched him eat every bite. Helping fix up the house he'd once taken such pride in would keep his mind off drinking, she'd reasoned, after she'd unearthed a paint scraper in the shed and gotten him started on the windowsills.

Right.

A good dose of winter cold was just the refreshing pick-me-up his teeth were chattering for. It didn't seem to be doing much for Jenn, either, as she wasted the day away on a yard he wouldn't be around in the spring to enjoy.

He'd agreed to let her keep coming round, mostly because it seemed so important to her. That and the fact that her Florence-Nightingale-on-steroids attitude was more interesting to watch than anything he'd seen on TV in years. But there was nothing interesting about the sadness of her frown today.

So, nothing was bothering her, huh?

Yeah. Him, either.

"I know *nothing*, darlin'. I've lived off it. And whatever you got on your mind, that ain't it."

"Well, whatever kind of nothing it is, I *ain't* interested in talking about it." She wielded the rake at a new pile of dead weeds.

"Looks to me—" he scraped and pulled and another shower of paint dusted both him and the scraggly hedges below the window "—like the kind of nothing that could drive a person to drink."

Her head snapped up. The rake hit the ground. "I want some water."

He watched her go, put everything into the next

scrape. Into not following. Into not caring what was eating at her or where his boy was at that very moment. He didn't care about anything anymore. At least he hadn't, not for a long time.

Damn, he needed a beer. He threw the scraper to the ground and jumped off the stepladder. His head screamed in protest. The world shifted off-kilter, and he clenched his eyes against the sharpness of the pain. Once the agony had faded, he stomped off after Jenn, the reminder of how little time he had left nipping at his heels.

A car screeched up the driveway before either one of them had made it inside.

"Jennifer Gardner!" A spitting angry Bob Carpenter leapt from the Cadillac. "What the hell do you know about my daughter being pregnant?"

CHAPTER NINE

"I'M SEVENTEEN, DADDY." Traci pulled another armload of things from her closet and wadded them into her suitcase. She was sniffling like a baby. *Daddy's little baby.* "I'm going, and there's nothing you can do to stop me. I can't stay here anymore."

She'd told her mom about the pregnancy as soon as she'd gotten home from school. Betty had promptly called Bob, then had curled up in a fetal position. The woman had been sobbing in her room ever since. Bob had arrived with Jenn Gardner right behind him. And so the interrogation had begun, complete with enough yelling to ensure the neighbors didn't miss a single sound bite.

Jenn, whose bright idea it had been to tell her parents in the first place, hadn't said more than five words. Bob was at his blustering, useless best. Traci's school rep was ruined—she'd been caught crying in the bathroom, then she'd run sobbing down the hall.

She'd never be able to face her friends again,

especially Brett. God, Brett. What was she going to say to him once he found out? And what about her parents' friends? The neighbors, most of them members of the church...

She dove back into her closet for more clothes.

She was so out of this place!

"I don't know what *Ms. Gardner* said to make you think running away is an option." Her dad's glower shifted to where Jenn stood beside the bedroom door, then back. "But you're not leaving this house!"

Jenn was following every word, but the woman only looked back at Traci and waited.

Coward.

Traci dumped another pile of clothes into the suitcase only to watch her father yank them back out and toss them beside the bed. He looked ready to drape her over his knee and paddle her, or cry.

The spanking would probably hurt less.

"You can't stop me from leaving." Traci returned to her bulging closet. Like her room, it was full of everything she'd ever asked her parents to get her.

So why did she feel so empty every time she was home? When was the last time she hadn't wanted to be somewhere, anywhere, else?

"Where are you going to go?" Jenn finally asked. "Back to the guy who hit you?"

"No." Traci threw the woman a *shut-up* glare as her father flinched. "I'll never be that stupid again."

"Then—" Jenn began.

"Who hit you?" Bob sputtered.

"I read a pamphlet at the clinic in Colter, all right!" Traci shouted at the room in general. "There are places I can stay—"

"Those are shelters for teenage runaways, Traci," Jenn said, all concerned calm when an impassioned defense would have been more helpful. "We're not talking about the YWCA. I've seen that kind of place, that kind of desperation and poverty. I've lived it. Running away isn't something you want to do on a whim."

"You're the one who said I need to think through my options. Well, I can't do that here." Traci grabbed more clothes, determined to do this no matter how terrified she was that Jenn was right.

It was time to face the truth.

"How long have you known she and Brett were sleeping together?" Leave it to her dad to focus on the most pointless thing possible. "If that boy laid a finger on my daughter—"

"The baby isn't Brett's," Traci said into the closet.

He grabbed her arm and pulled her around. "What do you mean it's not Brett's? How many boys are you sleeping with? Do you even know who the father is?"

Traci felt every warm thing left in her world evaporate. To her credit she didn't crumble. But the tears kept right on coming. Being back at school, wrapped around the disgusting second-floor toilet, suddenly didn't sound so bad.

She jerked free.

"This is why I'm leaving." She wadded the dress she held into a ball and threw it in the general direction of the suitcase. "Mom's so shocked she hasn't looked at me since I told her. And you think I'm a slut because I didn't buy into your lectures about premarital sex and abstinence. I can't think straight while you're stalking around glaring at me, and I need to think. I need to get out of here."

"And just where exactly do you plan on going? One of your friends? Every parent in this town will send you right back here. Count on it. The hotel will, too."

"See? You never listen to me! There are shelters, Daddy. I read about them at the clinic Jenn sent me to. You can't make everyone turn me away."

She glanced at Jenn, begging silently for backup.

"A free clinic!" He was in Jenn's face this time. "You sent my child to a free clinic? Just where the hell do you get off encouraging children to sleep around and defy their parents' choices."

"Stop yelling at her." Traci shoved aside the childish anger she knew deep down Jenn didn't deserve. "She's been my friend. Without her help—"

"Sounds like your *help*," he said to Jenn, as if

Traci weren't in the room, "was the last thing my daughter needed. She doesn't need another friend, Ms. Gardner. She needs responsible adults to keep her from throwing her life away. Did you know she was seeing this other boy?"

"Yes, I knew." Jenn stood toe-to-toe with the man when Traci couldn't even look him in the eye. Traci'd bet there wasn't much of anyone who could make the woman back down. "I tried to get her to talk with you and your wife. When she wouldn't, all I could do was make sure she had the information she needed to protect herself and her baby."

"All you should have done was inform Betty and me about our daughter's reckless behavior. Especially when you found out she was pregnant."

"If I had, Traci would have run away. Take my word for it. As it is, I've been able to get her to agree to counseling and prenatal medical care. And I've been able to talk her out of having an abortion until she's thought through her options."

"An abortion!" There was that look again. As if Traci were some slimy alien who'd invaded his home. "After everything we've taught you, you'd kill an innocent, unborn life?"

"What about *my* life?" She couldn't believe Jenn had said that. She wedged the lid of the suitcase closed and struggled with the zipper. "Don't I have any say in it?"

"No, not if you're considering an abortion. You can't be, honey…." So *now* she was his honey.

At least calling her a slut had been honest.

He tried to keep her from lifting the heavy case, but Traci sidestepped him and slid the bag to the floor. He reached to take it away, hesitated at her glare, then let his arm drop to his side.

"Don't do this," he said, sounding like her dad for the first time since he'd walked in the front door spoiling for a fight.

Traci stared at her trendy, high-top sneakers until her tears cleared. Then she rolled the suitcase toward the door. "I can't stay here, Dad."

"You're not going anywhere, young lady." All that gentle persuasion became cold, hard threat. "And you're not taking that car we bought you for your birthday. It's registered in my name, and I'll be damned if you're driving off in it like this."

"Fine! I'll walk."

"Please," Jenn begged as Traci passed by.

She didn't grab for her the way her dad had. She wasn't yelling. She'd always treated Traci like a grown-up old enough to make the decisions her parents thought they'd be in charge of for the rest of her life.

So Traci stopped.

"Wait in my car," Jenn pleaded. "Wherever you want to go, I'll take you. That's got to be better than walking in the cold."

Traci could have fallen at the woman's feet in gratitude. She glanced over her shoulder. Her father's anger and shock were gone. His confusion and hurt were worse.

"Okay," she said to Jenn, not wanting to go anymore but still unable to stay. "I'll be in the car."

And then what?

She ignored the internal jab. Blocked out the sound of her mother crying behind her parents' bedroom door. Thumping her suitcase down the stairs, she grabbed for the determination to get this over with. To finally not be hiding who she was from the people who were supposed to know her best. Good or bad, her parents knew the truth now.

Hadn't that been the whole point from the beginning of this six-month walk on the dark side? To push through the rules and their small-town beliefs, until her parents finally saw her. Dealt with her. Confronted the person they never dreamed she'd turn out to be.

She'd wanted to be treated like a grown-up. To experience the real world.

God, she was such a loser! They all were.

Winter slapped her in the face as she rolled her little-girl suitcase out her mom's custom-made-to-perfection front door. Her parents were so sure they'd taught her the important things.

Why hadn't they gotten around to telling her how much the real world sucked!

"WHO IS THE FATHER?" Bob Carpenter demanded. "Who did this to my daughter?"

"I don't know." Jenn's heart went out to the man. She'd seen that shocked, devastated anger in her own father's eyes. "I can't get Traci to tell me."

"What about all this help you've been giving her? You're supposed to be her new best friend or something!"

"I've been trying to advise Traci as much as she'll let me, without running her off. I can't make her take my advice any more than you can." She had to get Bob Carpenter to listen to reason, before Traci was gone for good. "Trying to force her to listen or to talk before she's ready will only make things worse."

"But you *can* tell her that sleeping around before marriage is okay, is that it? As long as you're respecting Traci's right to choose, it's okay to condone how she's lied to me and her mother."

"I've encouraged her to talk with you from the start, and I tried to get her to stop seeing this guy as soon as she told me about him. Sometimes teenagers have to make their own mistakes before they're ready to listen to anyone else."

He glanced to the soft sound of his wife's tears.

"Forgive me if I'm not impressed with the wisdom of your pop psychology, Ms. Gardner. Your negligence in not telling us what our daughter was up to makes you as responsible as this boy for what's happened to Traci. I intend to speak with your father about this. Your work with this town's youth is over. Mark my word."

"I already told my father I'm stepping down from working with the youth group."

"Joshua knows, too! Did no one stop to think that Betty and I should be involved?"

"He only knows that I thought it best for everyone that I not work with the Saturday group anymore. He doesn't know why."

Did Bob even realize he was blaming his daughter's situation on everyone but Traci? As if the girl wasn't capable of making any of the decisions she had—good or bad.

Jenn turned to leave.

"Jennifer…" His eyes pleaded, his expression lost. "Please. Talk my daughter into coming back home."

"I'll do the best I can. I promise."

She made herself walk away.

The Carpenters had to make their own choices, the same as their daughter did. The same as Neal and Nathan Cain did. She didn't know these people any better than she did the Cains anymore. She had no business doing anything but giving each one of them a chance to work their relationships and problems out for themselves, then getting herself out of the way.

Even if "out of the way" was a more excruciating place to be than ever.

Why you? Neal had asked yesterday. And he really hadn't known. Just as she'd always expected, he hadn't wanted to know anything about what her life had become, or what was important to her now.

Her heart felt like it was curling in on itself.

Get on with it, Jenn. Put yourself and your stuff on the shelf and find a way to keep Traci Carpenter in town. Do what you're good at. Stop torturing yourself by wanting more!

CHAPTER TEN

"GOD DAMN YOU for coming back here," Neal's father snarled after Neal let himself in through the unlocked kitchen door. "I didn't throw you out Saturday just to go through the trouble of doing it all over again."

The man was clean and sober today, but he'd lost a good twenty pounds in the years since Neal had last seen him. It would have been easier to spot on a smaller frame, but nothing about Nathan Cain had ever been small.

Certainly not his bitterness.

"And I didn't let myself get talked into coming back to this godforsaken place—" Neal used the dead-calm voice he reserved for condescending lawyers who assumed that since he was an ex-con, he'd crumble in the face of legal authority "—just to turn tail and run before we'd finished things."

"Oh, we're finished." When his father pushed away from the counter, his balance seemed to stay behind.

Neal caught him and helped him to a chair, mildly

shocked when nothing apocalyptic happened because they'd actually touched. Bolts of fire came to mind. Simmering brimstone, sparked by the unholy reality of the two Cain men sharing the same spot of earth again. Nathan was sweating, so Neal stepped to the refrigerator and pulled out a soda, popped it and handed it over.

His father looked at the can instead of at Neal. Drank and scowled at the taste of it. While he caught his breath, Neal glanced around the clean but threadbare kitchen. Every second in this place made him want to stay a thousand more.

"Why are you back here?" Nathan finally groused.

"This is still my home, isn't it?" Neal chuckled at the irony of his words.

Home.

The word had his mind leaving behind the familiar surroundings and thinking instead of golden hair and green eyes. Eyes that were a bit sadder now, worlds older than he'd expected, but no less beautiful than the girl from long ago. The girl he'd never really been able to stop wanting, needing, in a way he didn't want to need anything anymore. Especially now that he knew that the last eight years of her life had been an all-out sprint for survival, same as his. It bothered him more than it should that she wasn't there again with his father.

"This ain't no one's home no more." Nathan tore

open the lid on an oversized bottle of prescription medicine. With trembling hands he shook out two capsules and swallowed them dry.

He grimaced, then looked Neal dead in the eye for the first time. "You got something to say, then say it and get the hell out."

It was the same nasty tone the man had used in prison, when he'd given up and left for good. Igniting the same denial in Neal as before.

His father couldn't be dying. It all couldn't be ending. Not like this.

Don't let him shut you out again.

"So, what is it?" he asked, matching the man's cold stare. He was comfortable with cold, if that's what his father needed. "Cancer?"

Nathan cracked an honest-to-God smile. "That's what I always liked about you, son. You know when to can the sweet stuff and get right down to it."

It wasn't exactly a hug or a *bygones* pat on the back, but a weight subtly eased between them. They could do this ugly, or they could spare each other the melodrama. The ancient kitchen creaked, as if releasing a sigh of relief at their unspoken agreement to settle for plan B.

Neal eased into another chair and linked his fingers together, waiting for his father to make the first move. Same as he did with skittish clients who weren't sure they could trust anyone, least of all him.

"Brain tumor," Nathan finally admitted. "Inoperable. Terminal."

"A year?" Sorries or sympathy clearly weren't expected, no matter how desperately Neal needed to offer them. "Two?"

His father's head shook slowly from side to side. Something that looked like compassion flickered across his face.

"Months," he said. "Maybe weeks. No one knows, really. And I'm done with the pointless tests they wanted to keep running, just so that quack Harden can dig out all the gory details."

Damn.

Neal had almost put off this second trip back. Like he'd put off everything else he hadn't been ready to face. Still wasn't ready to face. What kind of man let the break between him and his father go on indefinitely, because absence was easier to deal with than repairing what they'd broken?

Now he could see the neglect he'd recklessly perpetuated for what it was—an appalling void he'd give anything to fill before it was too late.

"And Jenn Gardner?" Swallowing the question was impossible. "What's she doing here if there's nothing anyone can do?"

"Maybe there's something *I* can do." The tired,

sick old crank his father had become disappeared. For just a moment, Neal was looking at the man he'd once known. His *dad*. "Maybe helping me will finally convince her to let herself off the hook."

"Off the hook for what?"

"What the hell do you think!" And just like that, their Hallmark moment was over. The palsy in his father's hands was worse as he shoved his shaggy hair away from his eyes. "Oh, that's right. You've been too consumed with surviving your own nightmare to take a look at the ones you created with that stunt you pulled in the courtroom."

"I thought a trial meant weaseling out of taking responsibility for Bobby's death."

"That guilty plea was the most cowardly load of bull I've ever seen in a courtroom. And then you wouldn't let me file an appeal, or petition for early parole—"

"I thought I was doing the right thing."

It was the same old argument, and with it came the same flashes of nightmare. Bobby's head striking the cement curb. The blood. Neal's dad's tears, when he had quietly broken the news that it was over. That Bobby was dead.

Night after night. The same images had attacked him as he slept, until he'd finally stopped letting himself sleep at all.

"You took the easy way out!" his father shouted.

"Thinking it would kill the guilt. Like if you beat up on yourself and the rest of us enough, bled enough, you'd be free of it. How's that been working for you?"

Neal's jaw hurt from the restraint it took not to yell back. Yelling wouldn't change the fact that his father was right. He'd been a stupid, naive kid. He'd needlessly hurt himself and everyone who cared about him even more than they already were. Now his father deserved his say. And maybe they both deserved what he hoped would be possible next, after Nathan worked the pain and disappointment out of his system.

"Did you know she went and got herself pregnant?" his father asked. "That Joshua and Olivia tried to make Jenn give her baby up for adoption?"

Neal nodded his head, still reeling from all he'd read in that investigator's report.

"She'd been in trouble even before that." Nathan looked away. "Ran off about a year after your trial. Had the baby on her own. She somehow managed to put herself through college, I hear. Only came back for her mother's funeral, then after Joshua had a heart attack."

Drugs… Pregnancy… A teen runaway…

His Jennifer.

"She couldn't stand being in Rivermist after the trial, could she?" Neal felt physically ill. "So she kept doing whatever it took, until she finally had her excuse to get out…."

"Starting to sound familiar?" his father asked rhetorically. "Lord knows you could read the guilt all over her face in that courtroom. And when they handcuffed you and led you away, I've never seen anyone look so alone. She just sat there, poor little thing. Didn't move an inch. Her parents and everyone else got up and left. I couldn't stay anymore, either. Went off on a four-day binge, as I recall. But Jenn just kept staring at the closed door they'd taken you through. She was never the same after that."

"And now?" Neal couldn't keep himself from asking, couldn't keep the answer from being far more important than it should be. He slid to the edge of his chair. "How is she doing now? Is she… Is she okay? Is she happy?"

Nathan studied him, his full attention a startling thing. If Neal hadn't known better, he'd have sworn he saw a glimmer of approval in those eyes that looked so much like his own.

"She's got herself mired in another hell of a mess, if I don't miss my guess," his father said. "Seems to have a unhealthy attraction to lost causes. Buford tells me you do, too."

Neal's silence earned him a raised eyebrow.

"I called the man to chew him out for getting you down here," his father sputtered. "For over half an hour he wouldn't stop talking about you and that legal-aid center of yours."

And for over half an hour Nathan had obviously listened instead of hanging up.

"I...I didn't come here to talk about me." Neal knew he couldn't take that. Not today.

"God forbid." Nathan squeezed his eyes shut. Whatever medication he'd taken clearly wasn't making a dent in the pain. "Doesn't matter. None of it matters now. You want to know more about Jenn's life, you go ask her yourself. Whatever, just get out of my house."

If he'd said it in a rage Neal wouldn't have felt compelled to reach out his hand. Instead, his father sounded tired and lost. The need to touch, to reassure the man when Neal didn't have the first clue how, got the better of him.

"Get away from me, damn it." Nathan moved beyond his reach. "You came, you saw, now you're off the hook. I ran out on you when you were in prison. Now it's your turn to do the same. So stop yammering at me like we're old buddies. Stop showing up here like it's a reunion episode of *The Waltons*. I'm not wasting the last weeks of my life picking at a scab I can't even feel anymore."

His father's gasp of pain was what finally pulled Neal from the chair. Agitating the man wouldn't accomplish anything.

"Okay, I'll go for now. But I don't care how much of a bastard you want everyone to think you are, I'm not leaving town this time. I'm here because I care what happens to you, whether either one of us wants to believe it or not. I don't know what the hell we're supposed to do next, but I'll be staying at the Gables Hotel until we figure something out."

And he was headed back to the Gardners', damn it. He'd seen Jenn twice, and he'd selfishly been focused on his own problems both times. His father wasn't the only one who deserved the chance to tell Neal to go to hell.

He'd come back to Rivermist again to settle all outstanding debts. And if it killed him, that's what he was going to do.

"I WANT BOB AND BETTY CARPENTER over here now," Jenn's dad demanded.

"What? No!" Convincing Traci to stay the night at her dad's house had taken Jenn forever. Settling her and Mandy in the twin beds in Mandy's room after dinner had taken a half hour or so more. She'd promised the girl no one would force her to talk with her parents. "Traci won't see them. Not tonight."

"The child doesn't have a choice." Her father had been supportive up till now, but he'd pounced as soon as Jenn came down from tucking the girls in. "We've let her collect her thoughts. Gave her dinner.

Now it's time for her parents to take over. Bob started calling as soon as one of the neighbors saw Traci come inside with you. He'd be over here now if I hadn't asked him to wait."

"Traci's not a child. Both you and the Carpenters need to remember that. As far as the law and medicine are concerned, she's an adult who doesn't need permission to make decisions for herself and her pregnancy."

Hardball had never been Jenn's best negotiating tactic. Playing it tough with her own father felt like taking a turn at Russian roulette.

"Traci was on her way out of town," Jenn explained. "We either give her some space and the time to figure things out, or that girl's going somewhere else where none of us can help her."

Her father's hostile expression softened, no doubt with memories of Jenn's own destructive choices. The mistakes he hadn't been able to keep her from making no matter how much he pushed.

"Letting Traci stay here instead of making her go home removes the consequences of the choices she's making," he reasoned.

"She's pregnant at seventeen," Jenn shot back. "Trust me, she couldn't be more aware of the consequences she's facing."

"Bob's furious. He's talking about calling an emergency church council meeting for tomorrow. You're not that child's parent, Jenn. You need to—"

"No, I'm her friend." She hated that she was causing her father trouble all over again, in his town and his church. "If I betray Traci's trust by forcing her to talk with her parents I'll never get it back."

"I understand your reasons. And I can even respect them, given what you went through at her age." He didn't sound as if he wanted to understand anything. But there he stood. A little harried but talking calmly with her, one adult to another. Finally, *finally,* they'd achieved a modicum of mutual respect, and she was blowing it straight to hell. "I'm glad Traci felt like she could turn to you for help. But you can't honestly expect me to agree to something like this."

"I'll understand if you can't." Memories swamped her of the last time she'd seen him so unsettled. Of another conversation, full of pain and confusion, when her parents had explained through tears how giving their grandchild up for adoption was best for everyone. "I know this isn't fair to you. I just had nowhere else to take Traci tonight. We'll leave first thing in the morning if that's what you think is best."

"I don't have the first clue what's best right now," he admitted, "but I'm glad you felt like you could come here. Whether I agree with what you're doing or not, this is your home, Jenn. You and Mandy are my world. I want you to always feel like you can come to me, no matter what."

Her thundering heart felt as if it were shaking her from the inside out. Nothing he could have said would have meant more to her.

He cleared his throat, then turned to stare into the den's fireplace.

"Bob said you'd counseled the girl to have an abortion. That you'd been talking with her during some of the youth activities. I assured him that couldn't be true."

"I…" Her father defended her to Bob Carpenter? "I tried to talk her out of making a hasty decision about terminating the pregnancy."

"Bob's also convinced you know who the father is."

"I wish I did. She barely says anything about this other guy she's been seeing—"

"It's really not Brett Hamilton?"

"No." Memories of Traci's bruised eye collided with images of Brett's lopsided, homespun grin. "She wouldn't tell me who the father was, and she didn't want to see a doctor in town. The best I could do was bully her into going to see a friend of mine at a nearby clinic."

"Instead of calling her parents?"

"She promised to keep talking to me as long as I didn't. Otherwise, she was going to move in with the guy."

"And this boyfriend is where now?"

"Out of the picture."

"Before or after she got that bruise on her face?"

"They both happened right about the same time."

Her father's frown deepened. He was holding himself together, she realized. Getting all the facts. Erring on the side of believing her until she gave him a reason not to. She longed to throw her arms around him again, despite how terribly serious the situation was for both his career and the teenager sleeping upstairs.

"At least I know what's been on your mind the last few days, besides Nathan and Neal Cain." He sank wearily onto the couch. "How did you talk Traci into telling her parents?"

"I didn't." She shook her head as she sat, too. "I told her what I thought, how I'd felt in the same situation, but that she had to make her own decision. She went to her parents on her own. Traci's starting to take responsibility. Forcing her to go back home now could ruin that."

"You can't keep her from Bob and Betty forever, Jenn."

"I'm not keeping her from anything."

"That's not the way people around here are going to see it."

"Then I'd suggest people start looking at things a little differently. This is a woman with a lot to deal with, I don't care how young she is in years.

She needs our support, not her community passing judgment on what she's done. Why is it so hard to consider what Traci needs first, rather than what everyone else is going to think about it!"

She was wringing her hands. Staring at her lap. So unlike the professional she was supposed to be. Only the leftover frustration and pain of the misunderstood teenager she herself had been wanted to have its say. She looked up to see the worry on her dad's face.

"If Traci really wants to run away, you can't stop her," he said.

Jenn bit the corner of her lip against the fear that, come morning, that's exactly what Traci was going to do. "She already has a plan for where to go. I either convince her to stay with me, or she's on the next bus out of town."

Her dad rubbed his fingers across the fraying edge of one of the cushions her mother had covered herself. From out of nowhere came a deep, rumbling chuckle she hadn't heard in years.

"It definitely hasn't been boring around here the last few days." His smile washed over her. "I already knew it was going to be a challenge to make this second chance with you and Mandy work. But as usual, you've exceeded my expectations."

"Dad…" It was a priceless compliment. She had absolutely no idea what to say.

He leaned back into the couch.

"Your mother and I didn't listen to you when you were in trouble, did we? We couldn't stop wanting things back the way they should have been. Instead, we let them get more and more messed up."

"You and Mom did the best you could," she said, really meaning the forgiveness she was offering for the first time. "But we have a chance to do it differently for Traci. To help her and the Carpenters make better choices. And to do that, we have to do whatever we can to keep Traci and her baby safe."

Just a week ago, her father had said the exact same words, when he'd spoken about what he and her mother had wanted for Jenn. She held her breath. Said a silent prayer for the first time since she'd stopped believing prayer could make a difference in her life.

Her father stared for several long breaths, then his head gave a small nod.

"Keep the girl here for as long as you can," he said. "I'll call Bob back. Deal with him and Betty. Maybe after they give Traci a day or two to cool off, we'll be able to get the three of them together and figure something out."

He wanted them to stay.

He was saying *we*.

"But what about the church? This council meeting Bob is threatening…" The rumors were no doubt flying all over town. "Helping me means messing things up for you all over again."

"Oh, there'll be a mess." Her father's philosophical tone gave way to a wink. "But sometimes the biggest messes are the ones that finally show us our way."

She couldn't be sure, but she could have sworn he'd just called her his biggest mess.

A mischievous smile slipped out, the smile of a little girl goofing around with the father she loved with all her heart. "Glad I could help you out, Dad."

His chuckle wound down into a long pause. "Since we're exorcising the past and laying down bets on whether we'll handle *now* any better than we did *then*, you should know that Neal was here earlier."

Jenn found herself standing, not even sure why, except that running suddenly sounded like a fine idea. "He's back to see Nathan?"

"I got the impression he was here to talk to you," her father countered.

"He wants me to get involved in things between him and Nathan." She shook her head. "I told him I can't."

"But you wish you could?" Understanding filled her father's eyes. "Are you taking on the responsibility for fixing that relationship, too?"

"It's not that simple, Dad." Clearly, nothing between her and Neal Cain could ever be simple again. Certainly not how connected she still felt to him and Nathan after having nothing to do with either of them for years. "But I've got all I can handle with Traci. Neal will have to figure things out for himself."

The peal of the doorbell made them both jump. Her father's knowing expression as he left to answer the second ring said they'd made the same guess about the identity of their visitor.

"I'll be in the kitchen," he said as he led Neal into the den. "I have some phone calls to ma—"

"Mommy!" The sound of tiny feet thundering down the carpeted stairs was all the warning Jenn got. "Who's at the door?"

She felt herself falling into the startled depths of Neal's eyes, then she was enveloped in the sweet smell of her little girl's hug.

She'd dressed Mandy in a pink nightgown.

The color of spring.

Of eternal hope and renewal.

She cupped Mandy's tiny shoulders and pulled her beautiful child closer.

"Neal," she said to the one person she'd wanted to share her past with least, "I'd like you to meet my daughter."

CHAPTER ELEVEN

NEAL COULDN'T TEAR his eyes away from the picture of Jenn's daughter he'd found on the mantel above the fireplace. Reverend Gardner had hustled the child into the kitchen for a snack, but not before Neal had seen how perfect a reflection the little girl was of her mother.

"Your daughter must be at least…" He couldn't complete the sentence as he returned the framed photo to the mantel.

"Six," Jenn finished for him in a quiet voice. "Mandy will be seven in February. I had her about a year and a half after you left."

She sat on the edge of the paisley-printed chair, her shoulders drooping.

She's been through enough, Buford had said.

The investigator's report had noted a teenage pregnancy, the birth in a clinic in North Carolina. There'd been no real details beyond that and the extended break with her parents and the wild rebellion that had started soon after his conviction.

"And the father?" Neal flinched at the sound of the child's laughter from the other room. Another man's child. "Does he live in Rivermist?"

"There is no father." Her voice took on a cool edge, worlds more jaded than the Jennifer Gardner he'd once known. "At least none I've ever been able to pin down. I was a little—" she shrugged "—lost, for a while after you left."

Neal glanced once again at Mandy's picture.

"I know," he said. He knew the facts at least.

But nothing had prepared him for seeing Jennifer Gardner's child. Now knowing only the facts about her life wasn't nearly enough. Neither was just standing there, when he could hear the pain in her voice.

"You know?" She looked confused, appalled. "So you did read my letters. But I thought…I guess I figured since you never responded to any of them…"

"No, Jenn. I've never read the letters." Lying might have been kinder, but she deserved the truth.

"Oh," she replied, as if that settled everything. "I mean, I understand completely why you didn't." Her quiet, no-big-deal *understanding* cut through him. "You had every right to be angry, to blame me for what you were going through—"

"Blame you?"

"For being in that car with Bobby. For you going to prison." At his incredulous stare, she sat a bit straighter in the chair. "You stopped talking to me weeks before the hearing, Neal. You wouldn't even look at me. Take my phone calls. And I never heard from you after you left. If you didn't bl—"

"I loved you, Jenn." He said the words to her daughter's picture, unable to look her in the eye as he forced out the explanation she deserved. "But I was going to prison. I was too messed up about what I'd done to deal with anything else. I didn't know how to think about you, want to be with you and survive the rest…. I wasn't thinking about you at all. I had no idea what you were going through. That's why I came here tonight, to say I'm sorry. For everything you've been through. I never meant to hurt you."

"You still loved me?" Her mouth actually gaped open. "You're sorry?"

It was a toss-up which revelation had shocked her more.

"I'm not sure I was that aware of anything but surviving my first couple of years inside." The memories hardened his voice. "By then, my father had washed his hands of me, and I'd stopped getting your letters, and…I'd changed. I figured it was kinder to leave you two alone."

"Kinder! How could you have been so…so stupid!" Her eyes heated from pain to something else, then acceptance cooled them. "I died when you left. I lost everything, piece by piece. Threw it all away, because you were gone. Because it was all my fault."

"Stop saying that!" He knelt in front of her, longing to will into reality the peaceful life he'd always wanted for her. "None of it was your fault."

Her laugh was full of the kind of bedrock honesty he used when he told clients about his felony conviction.

"I was a whore, Neal. Why do you think Jeremy Compton was sniffing around me yesterday?"

"Don't say that!"

"I drank," she continued in a determined voice, as if she needed to purge the memories. "Did drugs. Slept with everything in pants. Took whatever I could get my hands on. Tried a hundred different loser ways to kill myself, because I was too much of a coward to end it cleanly for everyone. If I hadn't turned up pregnant with Mandy, I doubt I'd have survived."

"I know," he said again. "I have a file on all of it."

All she did then was blink back at him.

It blew most everyone's minds, her coming back here in the first place, after everything she's been through.

"I had it pulled together last night, after I got back to Atlanta," he explained. He made certain there wasn't a speck of judgment in his voice. He'd be damned if he let her believe he thought any less of her for the hell she'd fought back from. "There was a lot of shit in that file, but there were also notes about you getting your degree. Your social work with kids. You were a kid yourself, in pain and with no one to help you. I can't tell you how sorry I am for what you went through, but look at all you've accomplished."

Jenn gulped in several shallow breaths, emerging from the temporary insanity of discussing her past with Neal Cain. Of having him on his knees in front of her, saying he was sorry the same as her dad just had. She could waste energy being angry, but Neal had done what he'd had to do. She should be mortified, but she'd blasted him with everything—everything he'd already known—and he hadn't turned away. He was still there, trying to make her feel better, his compassion and understanding far worse than if he'd walked out in disgust. Because him staying made her want more. Way too much more.

"I...I'm sorry." She edged away and stood. "You came here to talk about your father, didn't you?"

His eyes narrowed as he stood, but it wasn't a stranger studying her now. It was Neal, his concern pulling on her emotions in that familiar way of dreams just before they distorted into nightmare.

None of it was your fault.

"I've already seen Nathan," he said. "I'm dealing

with him, what little he'll let me. I came here to talk to you. Because once I found out what you'd been through, I needed…" He shook his head.

"It's okay, Neal." She took his hand. Not because she wanted to touch him again, but because it was important that he believe her. That he stopped making her want to give him more than the clear conscience he'd come looking for. "I'm fine now. Mandy and I are doing great. You don't have to say anything else."

He squeezed her fingers. Looked so deeply into her eyes, she was certain he could see straight to her soul.

Don't go there, Jenn. He said he was sorry, and that's the end of it.

It had to be.

"Jennifer—"

"You should go." She stepped away from his use of her full name.

He followed. "Jenn—"

"Please," she begged through the panic building inside. The memories of loving him and losing him shrieked through her mind like opposing demons that would destroy everything they touched as they battled. "I need you to go."

She was going to scream if he didn't.

The phone's ring saved her. Pulled her back from both craving and dreading more of this man's attention.

"My dad and I are in the middle of something else, and…" *And I can't need anything the way I still need you.* "I have to go check on Mandy."

Neal nodded, relieved no doubt to flee her nonsense. He'd told her his story yesterday morning at the grocery. Now he knew hers. There was closure in that. A chance to move on. And as soon as he left she'd find a way to be grateful that he'd come back and given her at least that much.

"I don't know how things will go with Nathan," he said. "I'll stay for as long as I can. Try and get him to let me move back in. But who knows when that will happen, and he…he still needs someone watching out for him. Will you still stop by the house whenever you can…?"

It meant they'd run into each other again, but she'd made a commitment to Nathan. Her messed-up feelings for the man's son weren't going to be the reason she let him down.

"Of course," she heard herself promise.

Neal looked almost as if he wished she'd change her mind.

"Jenn, for as long as I'm here… If there's anything you need—"

"No!" she rushed to say, not caring how desperate she sounded. It was important that he not misunderstand. That neither of them did. "I'm fine on

my own. Really. Give your conscience a rest, and let
me live my life. You've got enough to deal with on
your own."

"YOU GOT NO IDEA just how good you have it, do you
girl?" Nathan asked the pesky teenager who'd invaded his kitchen.

Jenn had brought Traci over early that morning
when the girl had claimed she was too sick to go to
school. Morning sickness, for crying out loud. And
Jenn hadn't felt right leaving the kid at Joshua's all
day while she was over here harping at Nathan. Now,
for at least the next half hour while Jenn picked her
daughter up from school, it had fallen to Nathan to
supervise the sullen, really-needed-her-britches-
tanned teenager.

His own boy hadn't shown back up yet. Nathan
hoped that meant he'd hightailed it to that center of
his in Atlanta. The center that, by its very existence,
reassured him that Neal was going to be okay. No
one spending that much energy helping others,
whatever the reason, could stay lost forever. And he
wanted Neal to have his life back. It's all he'd ever
wanted.

"What's so good about any of this?" Traci Carpenter asked without looking up from the nonde-
script casserole Jenn had left instructions for her to
make. "Excuse me for not tripping all over myself

in gratitude because you haven't kicked me out yet. I know you don't want me here."

"You're right, I don't." He scratched the back of his neck. "But I'm not doing this for you."

Bob Carpenter had become a deacon at the church around the same time as Nathan. Now Nathan was a day-care program for the man's knocked-up daughter. Go figure.

"Then why am I here?" The girl was dressed in some pink excuse for a top and skintight jeans. If she didn't stop smacking her gum, he was going to reach in there and yank the wad out himself.

"Because Jenn's father's busy handling the fallout that came with helping you, and she needed some-place out of the way for you to spend your time. Lucky for you, I'm about as out of the way as it gets." A dying, unfriendly man Jenn hadn't spoken to for almost a decade was her only confidant in Rivermist besides her father. What the hell had happened to this town? "That woman's the best friend you're ever likely to have, so don't mess this up for her."

"Mess *what* up for her?" Several more smacks followed. "I'm the one who's pregnant. I'm the one the whole town's talking about."

"Why are your parents going after Reverend Gardner, if it's all about you?"

The girl gave a nonchalant shrug. "What's the

big deal? I'd have run away anyway whether he helped or not."

"Too bad no one in town's believing that but me." The girl could definitely benefit from a healthy spanking.

The fact that she was in his home at all was a testament to how much Jenn Gardner had come to mean to him in an unbelievably short time. There was something about the woman's bossiness, her determination to care about him when there was really no point anymore, that felt better than anything had in years. And that daughter of hers, Mandy.

He'd only met the child for a short time that morning, when Jenn dropped Traci off on her way to taking the little one to school. But like her mother, Mandy hadn't known how to be afraid of him. The two of them had become fast friends. She'd even asked if she could call him Grandpa Nathan.

Never figured on being a grandpa. It felt pretty amazing. In fact, given that his head was constantly threatening to throb off his shoulders, he felt closer to amazing than should be legal.

Jenn had managed to give him back a bit of what was left of his life, and he reckoned he'd do just about anything to repay her. But his newly discovered loyalty didn't extend to coddling other people's spoiled brats.

"Thanks to you—" He leveled a finger at the Carpenter girl "—the entire town's taking aim at Jenn and her father. Drumming up all the mistakes Jenn made almost a decade ago. Her working here with me—" not to mention Neal's reappearance "—ain't helping matters. The woman's got a battle on her hands, and it chaps my hide that you don't seem to give a damn about your part in it."

The child had the decency to swallow whatever sarcastic quip she'd been about to make. The moisture in her eyes threatened an oncoming flood.

"Don't you dare start feeling sorry for yourself." He grabbed one of the cans of condensed soup she needed for the mess she was making in the baking dish and shoved it at her. "Jennifer Gardner has a knack for knowing how to help people, even people like you and me who refuse to believe they need any help. So stop feeling sorry for yourself, and make her job a little easier, why don't ya."

"I'm not feeling sorry for myself." Traci wiped at her eyes with the ridiculous, fuzzy cuffs of her shirt. "And I know I need her help. Without her I'd be—"

"You'd be up a creek without a paddle, little girl." He saw reality creep into her eyes. "So I expect you to keep holding up your end of the bargain. Be where you're supposed to be, doing what you're supposed to be doing. Take care of yourself and that baby you're making. And get yourself to school, I don't care if you are feeling a little queasy. You can mope around there all day as well as you can here. And while you're at it, work things out with your parents before you make even more trouble for the Gardners."

Nathan Cain. Down-and-out bum and den mother.

The image was enough to make him smile.

With a grunt, he turned and stomped down the hall.

The front door swung open. Jenn trudged in, Mandy holding her hand and trailing slightly behind.

"But Mommy," the six-year-old said. "What did that lady mean?"

"Nothing, honey." Jenn began stripping the little girl out of her backpack, winter hat and coat. "It's nothing for you to worry about."

But from her posture he could tell Jenn was plenty upset. Why couldn't the people around here leave her the hell alone? And why wasn't her father running interference for her? Nathan had zero community clout anymore, but Joshua Gardner taking a public stand would go a long way for a lot of people.

"But what's everyone so upset with Grandpa about?" Mandy asked.

"Why don't you go see if you can help Traci in the kitchen?" Jenn gave her child's bottom a pat to scoot her down the hall. "You like stirring the chicken and rice, and I think there's a box of brownie mix in the pantry."

"Brownies!" The kindergartner took off toward

the kitchen, the hallway echoing with the sound of her tennis shoes slapping on the hardwood planks.

Jenn stood and shrugged out of her own winter gear.

"Catherine Compton was in the school office when I went in to get Mandy," she said, hanging her and Mandy's things on the coat tree beside the door. "She was talking with Nettie Hastings. She never looks at me, let alone speaks, but…"

"She decide today was the day to stir up the dirt between the two of you?"

"Not exactly." Jenn looked ready for battle. "She wanted me to know that she and the rest of the church council have called an emergency meeting tonight. The Carpenters can't get to their daughter through me, so they're going after my father's job."

CHAPTER TWELVE

"HELLO?" TRACI SAID after opening Mr. Cain's front door to the total stranger who had to be the man's son.

No one could look that much like the guy and not be related. And for days she'd been hearing the gossip that the notorious Neal Cain was back.

"Who...who are you?" He looked behind her as if he didn't really care.

"Traci Carpenter," she said. Like that would mean anything to him. "I—"

"I need to speak with my father."

"He...Mr. Cain's in the den, but he fell asleep watching the news." The grumpy old man must be really sick. Jenn acted like he was going to keel over any moment the way she fussed over him one minute and looked ready to cry the next.

"You want me to wake him up?" She let her eyes roam over the stranger's gorgeous face and the to-die-for body wrapped up in fitted jeans and a sweater. So this was the tough guy they said had killed his best friend at the homecoming dance, like a hundred years ago. The guy Jenn had been dating before she turned all bad girl and everything.

Her gaze came to rest on the leather duffel bag he held in one hand. "Um—"

"Is Jenn here?" Eyes the same dark brown as his father's locked with Traci's. "Maybe I can speak with her."

"I…um." Traci heard sneakers squeaking on the wooden stairs behind her.

"Who is it?" Mandy grasped the knob out of her hand and swung the door open until it bounced off the wall.

"Oh, hi," she prattled. "You're Grandpa Nathan's little boy. Are you going to the meeting with my mom?"

"I…What meeting?" the man asked Traci before staring back down at Jenn's daughter.

"The one where the church is going after Reverend Gardner, because of me." Ever since Mr. Cain had said the same thing, Traci hadn't been able to think of much else.

She'd finished making dinner, hadn't eaten much more than anyone else, and had dutifully cleaned up afterward. When Jenn left for the council meeting alone, Traci hadn't known what to say. What to do. Only she felt lousy now for not even trying to help.

"What did you do that has anything to do with

Reverend Gardner?" Nothing flickered in the guy's eyes as they locked back onto hers.

Cold.

She searched for another word as she gazed at him, but nothing came to her.

This guy was ice cold.

"I asked Jenn to help me, that's all." She dragged Mandy behind her and began closing the door. "I'll let her and Nathan know you came by—"

A large hand stopped the door and gently pushed until Traci was forced to move out of the way. The man's bag hit the foyer's hardwood with a thud as he stepped inside. He took his time studying the way Traci kept a squirming Mandy safely behind her.

The kid was slippery as an eel.

"Let me go." Mandy gave one final yank and succeeded in stepping around Traci.

"Not too close!" Traci jerked Mandy to her side once more.

The man kept staring.

Traci gulped at the size of the muscles bulging beneath Neal Cain's sweater.

"Where can I put my things?"

"You...You're moving in here?"

His eyebrows shot up.

"I mean, I know you used to live here and all, but—"

"Why don't we let Nathan and Jenn worry about

where I'm staying after I speak with her." He turned to go.

"Are you going to the church council meeting?" It was a meeting Traci should be at herself, except, according to Mr. Cain, she was too much of a loser to stand up and admit that she was to blame for all of this. "Can I come with you?"

"Why?" If the guy had actually looked like he cared, maybe she'd have hesitated before answering.

"Because I owe them. Jenn and her father. She's helping me think through what to do about my baby, and Reverend Gardner's helping keep my parents on a leash while I do."

Her hand smoothed over her stomach as she faced up to the opportunity Jenn was giving her. What all this was costing the Gardners.

Neal Cain seemed to be sizing up her age. That and the purplish bruise still shadowing her eye. With a nod, he turned to head out.

"So can I come?" She grabbed his sleeve.

He pulled his arm away as if she'd shocked him.

"Please," she begged. And not just because she was dying to ride in the bad-boy sports car parked at the curb. Something was churning inside her, something besides the baby making her sick every morning and half the day. Thanks to Jenn, and even grumpy old Mr. Cain, she cared about something besides her own problems for a change. Even worse, she was suddenly mortified that she hadn't all along. "Jenn shouldn't be standing up for her father alone. I should be the one explaining everything."

"Aren't you babysitting?" He glanced to where Mandy stood just inside the door.

The longer Traci looked at him, the warmer those scary eyes started to look. Especially every time Jenn's name came up.

Man, a few days with the woman and she was developing a bleeding heart of her own. A heart that felt good for a change, instead of like it was going to explode right out of her chest. Wanting to help Jenn and Reverend Gardner felt good. A whole lot better than obsessing about herself 24/7.

"Give me a minute to start a video for Mandy. She'll be fine in the den with your dad until I get back."

Neal stared beyond her at the den's curtained windows.

"Get your butt in gear." He turned away, almost as if he were worried he might head inside himself. "I'm pulling out of here in two minutes, with or without you."

She hustled back to Mandy and settled her with her favorite Disney movie and very clear instructions that she wasn't to leave the house. A quick note for the snoring Nathan was all that was left. Then she grabbed her purse and the designer jacket that didn't protect her from the winter temperatures as much as it went with her outfit, and headed toward the now-idling car and the blank expression of the man who was already behind the wheel. Gulping down lingering worries about his rep, she climbed inside.

He was a friend of Jenn's. Traci didn't care what the rest of the town said. If Jenn thought Neal Cain was okay, then he was okay with her.

"Before we get there," he surprised her by saying—she'd figured on a chilly, silent ride all the way into town "—why don't you fill me in. Exactly how much trouble are Jenn and Reverend Gardner in?"

"A CHILD'S FUTURE IS AT STAKE, and her parents should be guiding her in her decisions." Catherine Compton stood proud and tall as she addressed the church council.

She'd rallied behind the meeting, even though she wasn't a member of the council. She'd arrived with Traci's parents and a belligerent-looking Jeremy in tow, ready to discuss the latest flaw in Jenn's character, as well as why Jenn's father was partially responsible.

Jenn scanned the conference room. Half of Rivermist had turned out to watch the show.

"Reverend Gardner and his daughter have no right interfering in this family's ordeal," Catherine continued. "Simply because—"

"My father hasn't interfered with anything." Jenn ignored her dad's look of warning. He was sitting with the council, of course. They'd known tonight was going to turn ugly, and he hadn't wanted her subjected to it. He'd tried to talk her into staying away, into bringing Traci back to the house and waiting for him there. "He—"

"He has no more control over you now than he did when you were Traci's age," said the still-grieving mother who glowered at Jenn. "And now he's assisting you in ruining another teenager's life. How this council ever thought you'd be a good choice to work with our impressionable children, I can't begin to understand."

"I've resigned from coordinating the teen outings," Jenn said quietly, determined not to react to the growing tension in the room. Not to give anyone more reason to question her professionalism, or her father's for trusting her. "As soon as—"

"As soon as you decided you couldn't follow the dictates any qualified youth leader would." Catherine shook off her husband's restraining hand and pointed to Traci's parents, who were sitting to her right. "These parents should have been informed immediately of their daughter's reckless behavior. Instead, they were kept in the dark until their child decided to move out of their home—and in with our good reverend's family. And I hear she's spent today over at the Cain place, with that crazy old man."

"Sit down, Catherine!" Mr. Compton tugged her back to her seat.

Everyone in the room looked to where Jenn was still standing.

She stepped into the aisle between the rows of folding chairs and walked toward the front of the room. Metal chairs screeched as legs and bodies shifted to allow her to pass. A council meeting hadn't garnered this much interest since…well, since the last time her father's job had been on the line.

Shaking, she faced the council, gifted her father with a silent *I love you* along with a look she hoped he'd take as an apology, and turned to face her community.

"If this meeting were simply to discuss Traci Carpenter's situation, I wouldn't be here without an invitation, particularly since I haven't attended church here regularly since I was a teenager. But Mrs. Compton was gracious enough to speak with me at the school today, about the council discussing disciplinary action against Reverend Gardner. And I couldn't let that happen without setting the record straight."

She'd made her choices, wise or not. And she'd do exactly the same thing for any other child who needed her help. But her father had paid enough for her decisions. She scanned the sea of concerned faces before her, determination overtaking her anxiety. If she wasn't strong enough to stand before this town and own up to what she thought was right, what had the last eight years been about?

"The only thing Reverend Gardner is guilty of," she said in a firm voice she refused to let shake like the jelly her knees had become, "is putting other people's well-being before his concern for his job."

The truth in the statement settled on her like a bulletproof vest. Her father had chosen her this time. He'd put what she thought was best first. Quietly, with no fanfare and knowing full well that it would cause him enormous headaches, he'd taken a stand firmly in the chaos of Jenn's world.

Standing there, as the church council chatted quietly behind her, she felt less alone than she had in eight long years.

"He's allowed you to take advantage of your role as youth leader," Betty Carpenter said from her seat beside Mrs. Compton. Traci's mom turned disappointed eyes to Jenn's father. "Joshua, you let her keep working with the kids, knowing she was teaching them Lord knows what every Saturday. Certainly not what we as parents were trying to teach at home. Sneaking around. Lying. Premarital sex. Ab-abortion. My child wouldn't have considered doing any of those things if—"

"I've been doing those things for almost a year,

Mom," a quiet voice said from the back of the room, where Traci Carpenter stood with a determined expression on her face. "And if Jenn hadn't listened to me a few day ago, instead of lecturing me, I'd probably still be doing them."

"Sit down, young lady," Bob Carpenter said as both he and his wife shot to their feet. "This meeting isn't about you. It's—"

"If it's not about Traci, then what are we all doing here?" Jenn's father asked, speaking for the first time since the meeting convened.

The quiet rumbling of whispers that had been a constant background for the proceedings blossomed into ten conversations at once. Several prominent members of the community stood, as if height alone would give stronger voice to their opinions, either in support of or against what had been said.

"Everyone, please—" Mr. Hastings said over the melee. He was the head of the deacons and in charge of tonight's meeting. "Please, take your seats. And let's try and limit our comments to those who are called on by the council, or we'll never get out of here tonight."

When a veneer of order had returned, he focused his tired blue eyes on Traci. "Miss Carpenter, I think the reverend is right. Your insight into this matter is important. If you have something to share, we'd be happy to hear it."

Jenn wanted to cheer as the girl bravely walked

through the room full of people who'd known her since she was in diapers. She seemed stronger, somehow. More confident. Less afraid by the minute of the mistakes she'd made and the decisions she still hadn't. An amazing change, even if Jenn didn't completely understand where it had come from so suddenly.

Her smile faltered as a shadow in the hallway caught her eye—a shadow very much the size of Nathan Cain, who'd promised not to allow Traci out of his sight while Jenn was gone. Please, don't let the man choose now to make a scene in front of the town he'd thumbed his nose at for so long.

Traci glanced at the council members, the direction of her gaze settling on Jenn's father. Then she turned to look at her own parents.

"Stop being mad at Reverend Gardner, Mom. He's not the reason I lied to you and Dad." Jenn could tell the exact moment Traci spotted Brett Hamilton sitting in front of her parents. The girl's shoulders rose and fell, as if she were trying very hard not to cry. "He's not the reason I lied to everybody. Neither is Jenn—Ms. Gardner. She told me from the start I should tell you and Dad everything. She's the reason I finally decided to come clean…and to keep my baby…." She halted, as if the decision had just come to her as she said it. "To keep going to school, even though everybody knows by now, and they can't wait to talk about me. I'm going back tomorrow, Mom. I don't care how bad I feel."

Jenn curled her arms around the teenager and hoped against hope that her parents were listening. That everyone else would keep silent long enough for the words to sink in.

Who could have known that facing her parents in public would be easier for Traci than the face-to-face meeting Jenn had been lobbying for from the start.

"She's been busy today, even though she wasn't at school," Jenn offered when it seemed Traci had run out of words. "She was helping out at Nathan's. The man's very ill, and his house is in terrible shape." She let the reality of that sink in, daring anyone who happened to make eye contact not to feel guilty for the suffering being lived in their midst, with not a nod of concern from any of them. "She cooked him dinner tonight, and she'll be helping out more over the next few days. If he were a bad influence, I wouldn't let him spend time with my own child. And he's watching Mandy now, isn't he?"

Traci nodded.

"Thanks...thanks to Ms. Gardner," the teenager said to her parents, as if the rest of the spectators had faded away, "I'm finally starting to realize—"

"What you should be realizing, is that it's time to come home," Traci's father insisted. "This is ridiculous. Your place is with your family, not doing whatever you're doing with strangers."

"I've known Traci her entire life, Bob," Jenn's

father reminded the man. "I'm hardly a stranger. And I'm hardly unaware that the best place for her is at home, with her parents supporting her." He waited for Jenn to look his way. "But that's not always what families do. I am all too familiar with that reality as well."

"Joshua," Mr. Hastings said. "You're not actually—"

"I'm doing what I should have done eight years ago, but my wife and I were too afraid back then, and maybe too blind. I'm trusting my daughter. Jenn's helping a child no one else seems to be able to reach, and I support her one hundred percent. I'm fully willing to accept this council's decision—"

"My father's not the issue here," Jenn interrupted through a rush of tears. It was impossible not to remember another time, another public forum, when she'd been desperate for his support but so sure she'd never have it again. "I'm the one who took over the teen group, despite his warnings. The meetings have been successful up until now, but—

"We're very aware of your track record with this church's youth, Ms. Gardner." Mr. Hastings peered at her over the rim of his reading glasses. "But you must be aware that no one in this room is overly impressed now, given the current circumstances."

More half whispers surrounded them, like they had in that courtroom so long ago. Jenn made eye contact with as many people as she could, including Traci's parents and, unfortunately, Jeremy Compton.

People she was done cowering in front of.

Catherine Compton stood again, her manner more composed as she addressed Jenn directly.

"You're a horrible role model for the youth entrusted in your care. Your father could have stopped this months ago. Failing to tell parents when their children are taking part in inappropriate behavior is inexcusable. Taking the youth group out for burgers and heaven knows what else when you were supposed to be working with them at the church—"

"It was more than just going out for burgers," Brett Hamilton said from where he sat beside his father.

"Brett—" Jenn smiled her thanks, shaking her head at the same time. She could hear Traci catch her breath beside her. Brett's defense of the youth group's activities, considering he had every right to feel burned right along with Traci's parents, was as dear as it was unexpected. "You don't have to—"

"The youth outings are great." He stood, ignoring his father's disapproving frown. "Kids have been coming from all over the county."

"Brett!" Sheriff Hamilton, the man who'd handcuffed Neal and taken him off to jail, pulled his son back to his chair. "That's enough, son."

"I would have to agree." Mr. Hastings stopped fiddling with his pencil and sat forward. "I think I can speak for the council when I say we're appreciative to everyone, Brett and Traci included, for their insight into everything that's transpired. But this meeting was called to review Reverend Gardner's role in this situation, so let's stick to that, please."

"There's nothing to review." Jenn's dad's tone was equally calm and reasonable. "I've seen Jenn act responsibly, in my opinion, with regard to her position in this church. When it became clear her interests were in conflict with our views, she removed herself rather than causing strife within the congregation." He gave Jenn a nod, then his glance fell on Traci. "I've also seen her stand beside a scared young girl and refuse to let her leave town before she took the time to think long and hard about the consequences of what she was doing. And that same young girl is here tonight, standing up for Jenn. Even Nathan Cain is turning around under my daughter's care, if he welcomed Traci out at his place today just to take some of the heat off of me. How can I not support results like that?"

The room began to buzz again. Or was the static only in Jenn's ears? She gripped the edge of the conference table. Her dad, in his own quiet way, had just sided with her in front of God and everybody.

"You may be inclined to indulge your daughter," Catherine Compton said, "but that doesn't mean the rest of us have to. She's enabling that child's poor choices, despite the Carpenters' express requests to the contrary. And Traci and her own child's daily exposure to the town drunk isn't exactly cause for celebration."

"Don't lump everyone into one pot." Albert Perry stood at Jenn's right. He was a deacon and the owner of the local hardware store where Nathan Cain had once spent a small fortune on the home-improvement supplies needed to keep up his enormous home. "I, for one, think what she's doing with old Mr. Cain is just fine. I say we should be thinking about helping the woman, not punishing her father for the good she's done."

"She's teaching my child to disregard my wife's and my wishes." Bob Carpenter looked from Mr. Perry to Jenn's father. "And by allowing her to do it under your roof, you're as good as supporting the entire thing, Joshua."

"Stop talking around me, Dad." Traci stepped directly in front of her parents. "Try talking to me for a change."

"Come home, sweetie," Betty Carpenter reasoned. "Come home, and we'll talk about all of it. Let your father and me help you decide what's best."

Traci shook her head, standing straight and tall. But Jenn could see the tremor in her arms as she crossed them.

"That's exactly what my parents thought eight years ago, Mrs. Carpenter." She glanced another apology toward her father. "My parents tried to *help* me make decisions about my pregnancy. They did everything but listen to me. When I left, they waited for me to come to my senses and come back home. But that never happened. It often doesn't with pregnant teens on the run."

"And you're going to do nothing about this?" Catherine Compton demanded of Jenn's father.

"These aren't my decisions to make, I'm afraid," he said.

"Joshua, if you continue to support this behavior," Mr. Hastings said, "this council will have no choice but to—"

"Why doesn't the girl just stay at *my* father's house?" a voice boomed from the back of the conference room.

Everyone in attendance turned to find Neal Cain looming in the doorway. He stared angrily at Jenn, then with dawning shock at the room full of people now gaping at him.

"I'm sorry," he said to Jenn, who'd raised a hand to cover her gasp at having him appear as if out of nowhere to defend her. "I...I'm sorry."

Then before another word could be spoken, he turned and left.

CHAPTER THIRTEEN

THE ROOM ERUPTED in confusion at the spectacle of the town's blackest sheep making an unexpected appearance.

Jenn gave Traci's shoulder a quick squeeze, nudged the girl in the general direction of her parents, spotted Jeremy Compton headed her way with a less than friendly expression on his face, then she began pushing the other way through the milling crowd. Ignoring Hastings's demand for order, stumbling past chairs and people, she forced her way to the door and out into the hallway's dimness. She caught a glimpse of Neal as he slipped through the glass doors that led to the parking lot.

"Jenn?" Her father's hand fell on her elbow. "Did you tell Neal about the council meeting?"

"No. Of course not. I haven't spoken to him since last night."

"Yet, here he is, riding to your rescue." Her father's concern turned into a shocked kind of smile.

A smile that on any other father might have been a precursor to parental meddling.

"What? Dad—" But puzzling out what was going through his mind was interrupted by the meeting overflowing into the hall, more than one person motioning for her father's attention.

Jenn left him to his church politics and headed after Neal.

What *was* he doing here? And more to the point, why was it impossible for her not to follow him outside?

Yesterday she'd talked herself into being grateful for the closure they'd found. But after that display in the conference room—

Exiting through the same outer doors as he had, she turned the corner of the building and stopped short. His vintage Mustang was double-parked at the curb. Neal stood beside it, his back against the driver's door, hands in the pockets of jeans that looked just as amazing on him as his suit had.

He was like a living dream. The white knight her dad had joked about inside, standing right there in the shadow of the church that hadn't comforted either of them for years. Even in his jeans and sweater, he looked civilized. Successful. Tamed. But with his strong shoulders bunched as he stared up at the steeple, he was also every bit the angry young man people in Rivermist remembered.

He shook his head as she approached. "I'm sorry. I don't know what came over me back there. I came to talk to you, then everyone was on your case, and—"

"It's okay." It wasn't, of course, but she couldn't let him apologize for standing up for her.

He sneered. "Nothing's changed around here, has it? The town's out for blood, and they know just where to find the kind they like. What are you doing here, Jenn, putting yourself out there for them to take potshots at?"

"I'm trying to help a young girl and my father." What was *she* doing here? "Because Traci's pregnant, and because—"

"Because no one was there to help you when you needed it?" Responsibility clouded his features, the same as last night. "Because you know exactly how she feels?"

"Not exactly." But he'd hit the mark close enough. It scared her how close.

"Is that really Bob Carpenter's daughter?" At her nod, his humorless chuckle rumbled. "Bob Carpenter's daughter is knocked up and living with you at Reverend Gardner's. And just to add variety to your problems, she spent the day hanging with my outcast of a father. Something tells me I'm not in Kansas anymore."

"Nathan didn't have to agree to help."

"Between you and the girl, the man's collecting people the way he used to collect cars."

People, but not his own son.

Jenn glanced from Neal to his Mustang—Nathan's favorite vintage model, if memory served. The two of them had been restoring one similar to it together, so Neal could take it to college. They were going to spend Neal's junior and senior year remodeling the hunk of rust they'd brought home from that junk-yard....

"I...I think he's missed you." Neal's *get real* glare made it impossible for her not to continue, even though this wasn't her fight and everyone would be better off if she butted out. "If you don't believe me, you should take a look in your dad's garage. Or go see your room—"

"My room?"

"He's kept all your things there, exactly the way you left them." She hadn't been able to stop herself from peeking into Neal's room while cleaning the upstairs hallway that morning. And she'd never forget the shock of what she'd found inside. Or the moment she'd fully understood the depth of Nathan's pain, and what he'd sacrificed when he turned Neal away yesterday. "Everything's covered in dust now, but he hasn't parted with one bit of it."

Neal's shoulders rose and fell.

"You don't have to sell me on staying, Jenn. I

told you I'd keep trying." He seemed to be trying to convince himself more than her. "I know Nathan doesn't want anything to do with me now, but—"

"That's just it. I think he cares more than he wants anyone to know. He just doesn't want to trap you here. Underneath all that crankiness, I think he's more worried about what you need, and where you want to be. Why else would he keep all your things but not come after you when you got out of prison?"

The look that flashed across Neal's face reminded Jenn of Traci, when the girl told her parents she was willing to leave—but Jenn had been certain what she really wanted was for someone to make her stay.

"Why are you here, Neal?" she asked. "Instead of home with your father?"

"Nathan was sleeping." At her disbelieving look, he gave her a good-ol'-boy shrug she remembered all too well. "When Traci told me about the meeting, I…I needed to see you."

"You needed to see me…. At church?"

His scowl gave way to a sigh. "I knew what was going to happen here. I left you to face crap like this on your own once before. If I can help now…"

To her rescue her father had said. Fast on the heels of the daydream image came the same panic as yesterday. Having him here, here for her, meant losing him again.

"You… You should be focusing on Nathan." She didn't remember either of them moving, but he was closer. "He's the reason you came back to Rivermist."

Neal was shaking his head in that absent way he had when they were kids and he'd been lost in thought.

"What if Nathan's not the only person I want to help?" The expression in his eyes was suddenly that of the boy she'd lost, rather than the stranger who'd walked back into her life. "I'm a fighter, Jenn. I discovered that in prison. But I never fought for what I wanted most. For the things I lost here. Lord knows, I've tried hard enough to stay away. And look at how much pain that's caused."

"But you're here for Nathan, now. That's what's important." She clutched his arm, needing him to believe her. "You should be over there now, not here with me."

Neal held tight when she tried to inch away.

Where was the cold stranger who'd showed up yesterday?

"Nathan's not the only one I hurt." His hand cherished her cheek. His fingers were tracing the highlights in her hair. "I thought forgetting you was the right thing to do," he said. "So I stopped feeling anything at all. Now being here, being next to you and seeing everything I threw away—"

"You didn't throw me away." Her hand found his chest. Her fingers actually tingled. "You went to prison, and it was a long time ago. You have to stop feeling responsible for things that aren't your fault."

It was a lesson she'd yet to master herself, but she'd preach it to him, regardless. Whatever it took to not keep from circling back to this every time they saw each other. She couldn't take much more.

His hand covered hers. "I didn't mean to leave you alone, Jennifer. I thought you'd have your family...your future."

"Future?"

Without him?

He gently pulled her closer.

"Don't!" She put more conviction behind moving away.

Where they were, what was at stake inside the church for her father and Traci Carpenter, was where Jenn's attention should be. But Neal held firm, the familiarity of his touch as hypnotic as the deep pitch of his voice.

"Is it so terrible that I want to help you?" he asked.

It was devastating.

"You... You don't know what you're saying."

Taking comfort and concern from others wasn't her strong suit. From this man, it would mean disaster.

"If you think these people are out for my blood,"

she reasoned, "what about you? Do you have any idea what you'd be getting yourself into, jumping into the middle of my problems with the Carpenters?"

"Probably not." His chuckle sounded so much like Nathan's. "And I usually make a habit of being the one person in the room who knows the most about whatever's going on. But as long as you're part of it, I think I'd be willing to get into just about anything. You were amazing up there in front of that room of vipers."

The pride in his voice completely did her in. His instinct to care about her, after every unfair thing he'd been through, clutched at her heart. Terrified her.

"You're an amazing woman, Jennifer Gardner."

Muscles along his jaw flexed, reminding her of just how good it had felt to kiss all that strength. How long she had needed just one more taste of what she'd never found with the countless boys who'd followed him.

And then his lips were brushing hers with soft, gentle, almost-nothing kisses that were all the more erotic because of the fierceness of the memories and emotions igniting between them.

"Stop. Please," she begged, tears breaking through the beauty of the moment. "I can't."

"Jenn?" He was still holding her, still making her want this. "Don't—"

"I can't." She pushed against the immovable strength holding her so safe and close.

"Get your hands off her, you son of a bitch!"

Jenn was ripped out of Neal's arms before Jeremy Compton's words fully registered.

"You've got no business here, Cain." Jeremy slid an arm around her.

Dislodging herself would have made more of a scene, so she settled for shooting him a nasty look as more and more people exited the church to watch the spectacle.

"Actually, this is *none* of your business," she said. The proprietary way he was holding her was creepier than usual, considering the hateful stare he'd shot her inside.

"Did he hurt you?" Jeremy turned until his back was to Neal. His arms circled her waist as he took stock of her from head to toe, like a man checking his car for damage after a fender bender. "I know my mom was rough on you in there, but no one wants you spending time with this guy. Do you want me to take care of him?"

"And you'll what, Jeremy?" The way Neal pitched his voice no one beyond the three of them could hear. "Manhandle Jenn some more, just to piss off me and your mama?"

Sure enough, Catherine had joined the growing circle of onlookers, her hand covering her mouth in shock at the sight of her baby talking with the town outcasts.

"I don't give a damn what my mother thinks." Jeremy rounded on Neal. "No one wants you here. I'm sure Jenn and her father have no interest in your help. I don't know what you think you were doing in there, but you're just making things harder for everyone."

"I'm making things harder?" Neal's expression turned arctic cold as Jenn tried to step around Jeremy, only to have the younger man restrain her once more. "Looks to me like your assistance is the last thing the lady wants."

"What I don't want, is to be talked about like I'm not standing right here." A stomp to Jeremy's instep allowed her to finally move away. The sight of Neal squaring off against Bobby's kid brother had shot what felt like ice water through all the warmth his kisses had left behind. This wasn't going to happen. Not again. "I'm a big girl. I don't remember asking anyone for assistance of any kind. So back off, both of you. You boys aren't going to get into it on the church lawn, not over me."

She caught the half smile teasing Neal's lips. A quick *atta-girl* nod of respect. The tension eased from his powerful frame.

"Don't tell me you're falling for this guy." Jeremy sneered at the look that had crept across her face. "I was right. One whiff, and you're using his sick old man, your problems with the Carpenters and this town, whatever you can get your hands on, to get back in his pan—"

"You never did know when to shut up, Jeremy." It was like Neal was channeling the brilliant attorney his father had once been, the way his voice smoothed out and his tone made it sound as if he was talking about nothing more titillating than the evening's weather.

But the bite of each word was evidently too much for Jeremy. He hurled himself forward, his fists driving straight toward Neal's face. Neal's lightning-quick reflexes as he sidestepped the blow, Jeremy's growl as his forward momentum caused him to trip and topple to the ground, shocked everyone, Mrs. Compton most of all.

"Oh, dear God!" she shrieked as she ran up to the scene that must be straight out of her nightmares. "Stop it!"

Gasps escaped from the growing crowd as Jeremy lurched back to his feet, battle-ready for a second pass. Jenn stepped forward, intending to hold him off. Neal hadn't so much as raised his hands in defense.

"Guess that's my cue to leave," he said, straightening the sleeves of his sweater as if he'd done nothing more than swat away a fly. "I'll see you and Traci back at my father's, Jenn."

He didn't bother to look at Jeremy as he eased with quiet dignity into his car and drove away. Rivermist's most dangerous son now carried himself with the sophistication of the businessman no one here had ever dreamed he'd become.

"Do you really think I should stay with Mr. Cain?" Traci asked. She stepped closer, her parents following. "Would you move over there with me if I did?"

"I—"

"You can't be serious!" Jeremy said.

"Absolutely not!" Traci's father concurred, as Jenn shot Jeremy a look to get lost.

"Dad!" Traci rounded on her father as Jeremy skulked away. "If it'll keep me from making more trouble for Reverend Gardner, then—"

"You are not staying with that old drunk. Think about the safety of your baby, if not yourself. There's no telling what Cain might do."

"Nathan Cain isn't—" Jenn began.

"He's not a drunk, Dad. He's sick." Traci breathed in a sniffle, but she didn't back down. Holding her own against her parents was such a major victory for Traci, Jenn wanted to cheer. "And you should be thanking him instead of talking about him in front of half the town like he's a menace. He's part of the reason I came tonight. I think spending the day with him actually helped me think some things through."

"Helped how?" Betty Carpenter asked, restraining her husband. "What is he doing…?" The woman gestured at Jenn with the hand not holding her husband's arm. "What are *she* and Reverend Gardner doing that your father and I can't at home?

"They listen to me, Mom. They treat me like a grown-up instead of like I don't have a brain in my head." A fresh batch of sniffles sprinkled the discovery in Traci words. "And they're letting me figure this out, instead of telling me what to think, no matter how hard it's been on them to have me around."

"It's been wonderful, honey." Jenn squeezed her shoulder, feeling the truth of her statement. This was the payoff she fought for, when a young woman's eyes finally opened to all she could still have instead of all she'd lost. This was her reward for whatever else in life *she* couldn't have. "Mr. and Mrs. Carpenter, you should be very proud of your daughter. She could have left at any time. She didn't have to stay today and help Nathan, or come here tonight worried about my father and me."

"She didn't run away?" Bob snapped. "That's the high point of your day helping her *figure things out? Is that supposed to reassure us?"

"No, it's supposed to show you that I'm not hopeless." Traci's little-girl voice was back. "To convince you not to turn the entire town against the people helping me just because you can't have your way."

She took off, running past where Jenn's father stood on the fringes of the milling crowd.

"H-has she said anything else to you about keeping the baby?" Betty Carpenter asked Jenn, her attention divided between her husband and watching her daughter disappear through a crowd of friends and neighbors.

"Just what you heard inside. That she's decided not to have an abortion." Jenn squared her shoulders as her father and Catherine Compton stepped closer. "I think she's making real progress."

"Progress!" Catherine repeated, wiping at the tears that had erupted at the sight of her son and Neal nearly coming to blows. "Coming from you—"

"Stop it, Catherine!" Jenn's father demanded. His biting tone was such a rarity, everyone within earshot stared. "I'm sure the Carpenters appreciate your concern, but criticizing my daughter isn't helping anyone. Bob, Betty, I'm asking you as a friend not to make the same mistake Olivia and I did. You have a chance to listen to your child before it's too late, before things are taken even more out of your hands. Don't turn this situation into a play for power, when it should be about loving your child the best way you know how."

He turned to Jenn.

"If you think it's best to move with Traci to

Nathan's," he said, "then you have my blessing. Assuming the man's even willing. I'll miss having you and Mandy at home while you're gone. But I trust your judgment, honey."

The small pat he gave her before walking away had the impact of a full body hug. Whatever she chose to do, he'd support her. Period. Just when she wouldn't have minded his advice…

Move into the Cain house? With Neal? If in fact his father let any of them stay.

"Jenn?" Betty Carpenter asked. "What are you going to do?"

Jenn gave Traci's worried parents her full attention. "I'm going to ask Traci what she needs, and do whatever I can to support her. Why don't you plan on stopping by? I think she'd be more than willing to talk with you again, if it were on more neutral ground."

"Neutral ground, where?" Betty asked.

"Does it matter?" At least Neal's impulsive offer had gotten the Carpenters' attention. "As long as you and Traci are there together."

She had to wonder if Neal Cain's return to Rivermist hadn't been just the shake-up their picturesque snow globe of a town needed to help everyone refocus on what was really important. And since she could still feel the feather-light touch of his kiss on her lips, clearly she was the one most shaken of all.

NEAL STOOD in his father's garage, Jenn's words ringing in his ears.

I think he's missed you.... He's kept all your things...exactly the way you left them....

He'd even kept the damn car.

Not only that, the man had rebuilt the '66 Shelby GT to vintage perfection, right down to the glossy blue top coat and center white racing stripe. It must have taken him years on his own. Neal glanced over his shoulder at his own car. He'd busted his ass doing the detailed work restoration required. Methodical work that he'd looked forward to day after day. Because doing it, and then driving the finished car, had been the closest thing he knew he'd have to sharing the experience with his father.

Nathan's Oldsmobile sat in the back of the driveway under the rusted-out basketball hoop, it's paint faded from the sun. But the Shelby, the one he'd bought for Neal, was tucked carefully away in the garage.

Headlights flashed up the drive, heralding the arrival of the woman he'd thought he'd never share anything with again, either. Certainly not the sweetest kiss he'd ever known. The woman that couldn't bear the thought of finding happiness in something as perfect as their kiss, yet she seemed at ease taking the problems of the world on her shoulders. Proving to everyone, most of all herself, that she wasn't the miscreant this town had labeled her.

Watching her from the shadows at the church council meeting had changed him. Simple as that. He'd lost forever the ability to relegate Jennifer Gardner to his memories as a sweet, young girl. She was all woman now, mesmerizing in her passion for whatever and whomever was lucky enough to have her support. She'd blown him away, making him briefly think they could take the world on together. He'd been an ass, saying what he had in front of half the town. Stirring that snot Jeremy up. Causing a scene. But he'd meant every word. If moving in here with the Carpenter girl was what Jenn needed, then that's what was going to happen.

"Mommy!" Jenn's little girl called. She flew out the kitchen door and hurled herself into her mother's arms.

Jenn hugged her close, cupping the child's head to her breast and kissing the golden curls at the girl's temple. Neal should have left the garage's shadows and let them know he was eavesdropping, but the shadows were what he liked best—just like when he watched Stephen do his thing in court. He'd sit in the back watching, analyzing, learning. But never getting too close to the lives being played out on the courtroom's stage.

Besides, the scene before him was too surreal to

interrupt. A glimpse into Jenn's life he'd thought he hadn't wanted, but now couldn't look away from.

The daughter whose conception and birth had caused Jenn so much trouble was clearly the center of her world. The teenager whose problems had become Jenn's in a very public way tonight was by her side, where Jenn refused to let anyone tell her the kid didn't belong. And as she held those she cared for close, he realized that before his return to Rivermist all he'd known how to do was push people away. Now...

His visit to her father's last night should have been the end of it. Jenn needed him to move on. Only he'd had to see her again today. Had to help her. To touch her. To have her closer...

He thought of her letters he'd brought back from Atlanta. Letters he'd brought for her, hoping it might bring her some peace to know he'd kept them. Only he hadn't been able to part with them last night. As long as he had her letters, at least a piece of Jenn was still his.

"It's about time you got back," his father grumbled, slowly joining the group outside. His steps dragged as if each one caused him pain. "What happened at the—"

Neal watched his father catch sight of his Mustang, illuminated by the lights that kicked on every time someone came up the driveway. Watched some of the fatigue ease from the man's body as he stood taller, anger and maybe a little bit of hope settling on his face.

"What the hell's going on out here?"

Another car screeched to a halt at the end of the drive.

"Stop right there, Jeremy," Jenn said as she set her daughter aside and stepped away from the group, taking the jerk on by herself.

"Where's Neal?" Jeremy demanded as he moved farther into the light shining down from the roof. "Is that his car?"

"That's none of your business. Nothing that happens here, to me or Traci Carpenter or Neal and Nathan Cain, none of it is any of your or your mother's business. So stop butting in. Stop trying to protect me from something you don't understand. Stop following me all over town, or I swear—"

"Following you!" Nathan, his knees cracking, his head clearly aching, stepped between Jenn and a man more than twice her size. Neal, who should have been intervening, could only stare, mesmerized, at the sight of Jeremy Compton cowering away from Nathan's imposing height. "Are you part of what's had this girl spooked the last couple of days? Then let me tell you what's going to happen the next time you get anywhere near her—"

"Nathan, please. I'm fine." Jenn gave the best imitation of "fine" Neal had ever seen, catching

Mandy to her side as the little girl crept closer. "I can handle him."

"You think so?" Jeremy's smile was all bully. "You and Neal, you gonna handle me together, is that it?"

"I don't need anyone's help to handle your messed-up infatuation with me, just because we knew each other as kids."

"Knew each other?" The man's laugh raised the hair on the back of Neal's neck. Jenn stiffened, but she didn't back down. Her courage was the only thing that kept him in the shadows. No way would he take away her chance to verbally kick Jeremy Compton's ass to the curb. "Is that what we were doing your senior year in high school—getting to know each other? You ever tell your kid there just how well you *knew* half the boys in the county? How any number of them could be her daddy, even me? Is that what you're going to be doing with Neal to-night—getting to know him all over again?"

"Mommy?" Mandy asked, when Jenn couldn't seem to form a comeback.

Jenn lifted her hand to her throat as if she were about to vomit.

"You better get that filthy mouth of yours back in your car and the hell out of my driveway." Nathan shoved the kid's shoulder, knocking Jeremy back-ward. "Go on, get!"

Whether from shock at Nathan's strength or satisfaction at finally blasting through Jenn's defenses, Jeremy backed away. But he threw himself into his car with the air of a man who hadn't had his last say.

"Are you okay?" Traci slipped a supportive arm around the woman who'd just done the same for her at the church.

"Mommy?"

"I…I'm fine," Jenn croaked, coming out of her trance. Nathan grunted as he stepped toward her, but before he could speak she crouched and pushed her daughter's bangs from her eyes. "Really, sweetie, I'm fine."

Only her voice still sounded too far away. Too broken by the sickening idea of Bobby Compton's brother possibly being her child's father.

"Jenn?" Nathan persisted. "What—"

"Why don't you take Traci and Mandy inside?" she asked. Her voice trembled only slightly. "I picked up some ice cream at the grocery this morning. Chocolate. Mandy's favorite."

"Jenn." His father hesitated, the compassion in the single word filling Neal with envy.

"Please." She was pleading now, where she'd been nothing but piss and vinegar with Jeremy. She glanced to where Neal still stood inside the garage, then back at his father. "I—I need to be alone for a few minutes."

Nathan eyed Neal's car again, looked around the yard and then at the garage. Then he shook his head and started back toward the kitchen.

"I suppose you'll want ice cream, too," he groused at Traci. "While you eat, you can damn well tell me what happened at the church."

Jenn started to say something to their retreating backs, but she let them go. Walking a few short steps, she eased onto one of the benches beside the picnic table that had been the first thing Neal and Nathan ever built together.

His mom had always loved picnics.

"How much did you hear?" she asked without turning in his direction.

"All of it." He stepped out of the shadows and sat beside her, propping his arms on his thighs and locking his fingers together. How else was he going to stop himself from pulling her into the hug he just might need more than she did? "Could Jeremy be your daughter's father?"

He hated the way she flinched. But if she didn't want to talk about it, why had she stayed outside when she knew he was there? Once upon a time, they'd been able to talk about anything.

"I suppose it's possible, but…" She looked up at the stars. "He's never said anything about it before. He's always been a little too interested in hooking up, but nothing this aggressive…." She spread her hands in front of her, as if to ward him off again. "Nothing this possessive, not before…"

"Before I came back?"

And jumped right into the middle of her problems.

"I should head over to the hotel," he said. But before he could head inside for the bag he'd left, her hand clutched his arm.

"You're not leaving." The same fierceness she'd shown Jeremy now flashed at him. "You need to work things out with Nathan. Traci and I will go. We should be getting back to my dad's, anyway."

"I thought you wanted the council off Reverend Gardner's back." Turning toward her was a mistake. Their thighs brushed. Her sweet face was only inches away. He was worlds too hard for her, but when she was this close he felt like the boy she'd loved. Like the last eight years were gone and he still had a right to want everything they'd once had. "You and the Carpenter girl staying here will do that."

She nodded, then she shocked the daylights out of him by taking his hands in hers. Back at the church, she couldn't get away from him fast enough.

"You've already done enough for me, Neal, just by saying what you did back at the meeting. Even if Traci and I don't move in here, you got her parents thinking. Maybe closer to being ready to listen." She let go of his hand with a hesitation he couldn't be sure was real or imagined. "Besides if Traci and I stayed here, we'd be shining the community spotlight right on you and *your* father. Especially with Jeremy acting the fool like he did tonight. You two don't need that kind of distraction. There's so little…so little time left. You can't afford to waste any of it."

He trailed his fingers up her arms until his hand cupped her beautiful face. She had it all figured out, what everyone else needed.

What did she need? What did she want?

Could it ever again be him?

"Didn't you see my dad a minute ago?" He feathered another kiss across her lips, just once, then twice, before he lost the nerve, and the chance, forever.

"Your… Your dad?"

She didn't kiss him back, but she didn't shy away this time. If that was all he had to live off of for the rest of his life, he'd die a lucky man.

"He was a dad again tonight." Neal forced himself to inch away. Forced himself to focus on what was important to Jenn. "Not my dad, but yours. He cares about you. Traci, too, if I don't miss my guess. If anyone belongs here it's you. Look at what you've done for him in just a couple of days. Let him help you. Let me help you by getting out of the way."

Lucky for her that's what he did best of all.

"What Nathan needs is you."

He made himself stand and tugged her hand until she was beside him. "I'll just be a mile away at the hotel."

"You need to be in your room here," she argued, making the need to see his old things, the things his father hadn't been able to part with, burn even brighter.

"Not an option." Then he turned away from what he'd finally accepted he needed most of all—her.

CHAPTER FOURTEEN

"You mean to tell me, you weren't even going to ask me to take the girl in?" Nathan thundered at Jenn in the kitchen a few minutes later. He'd carefully avoided looking in his son's direction since Neal brought up the subject of Traci moving in.

Jenn glared at Neal for starting this. "I didn't think you—"

"What? That I wouldn't help you after everything you've done around here? Not that the Carpenter girl's likely to stay, even if I offered. We didn't exactly have a pleasant visit while you were out today."

"I'll stay if it makes things easier for Jenn," Traci said from the doorway. She had Mandy with her, and it was anyone's guess how long the two of them had been standing there.

"It's not that I didn't think you'd help." Jenn kept her voice low and even, made all the harder by the nearly impossible-to-resist urge to scream. Jeremy's explosion. Neal's kiss. And now the Cain men were ganging up to *help* her? "It's just—"

"It's just that taking on the world alone is a whole lot easier than letting anyone do anything for her," Neal said, finally earning himself Nathan's attention.

"Well, that's just too damn bad." Nathan spun toward Jenn so fast he swayed, his balance becoming more of a problem by the day. Not that it had stopped him from putting his body between her and Jeremy. "You got me out of the bottle and sober enough to care about what's going on around here. Now deal with it. If I want that girl to stay here, and she's willing to do it for you, then it's a done deal!"

"If not, I'm leaving town like I planned all along," Traci insisted. "I've caused you and Reverend Gardner enough trouble."

"I'd have to move in here with you," Jenn reasoned. "And that's not—"

"Fine by me," Nathan said. "Why not?"

"What? No!" How could the drunken man she'd nearly run over a few weeks ago be offering to spend his last days on earth helping shelter someone else's child? "I can't ask you to do that."

"You didn't. I'm offering. Do you want to keep that kid in Rivermist or not?"

"But you and Neal. You need—"

"I need sleep." Nathan headed for the hall stairs with a less-than-steady gait.

Neal watched him in silence.

"But…" She trailed after the old man.

"Don't you finish that sentence." Nathan stiffened as Neal joined them in the hall. "Damn, girl. After everything you've done for me, don't you dare think about not letting me do this for you. If I want to thumb my nose at the tight-ass people in this town to give you and your old man a break, humor me."

"Don't do that, Nathan," Jenn warned. "Don't yank Traci around out of some personal need to annoy the church council."

"Well, I wondered what it would take to get you to call me Nathan." The man had the nerve to laugh.

"I'm serious."

"So am I."

"You're encouraging a pregnant teenager to make even more trouble for herself by moving in here when it's not necessary?"

"It is necessary. For you. She's not going to stay with Joshua anymore. Not after the scene she said played out at the church tonight. It's either me or a bus out of town. If she wants to do this for you, let her!"

"*I'm* not the point here."

"Well maybe you should be for a change." Nathan pointed toward the kitchen. "You've busted your butt for that girl in there. Let me take a watch or two."

"You're trying to tell me you care what happens to Traci Carpenter?"

"I care what happens to you. And you look like hell. You keep going like you are, something's going to break. And I'm not going to sit around while that happens."

"Neither am I," Neal agreed.

Nathan stared at his son, then gave him a nod of silent agreement. The first honest, nonhostile emotion she'd seen pass between the two of them.

Jenn felt her smile all the way to her toes.

Gotcha!

"If I stay, you stay, too," she said to Neal.

"What!" the two men demanded in unison.

"It's the only way I'll agree to this madness." She cast a warning glance at Traci as the girl joined them in the hall, asking her to be still. "Neal thinks he'll make trouble for me if we're both here. But I'm not going to be the reason he spends another night away from this house. You two share the same roof, or Traci and I walk."

She'd never been very good at bluffing. She prayed that she could pull it off just this once. Nathan was right. She couldn't let Traci leave Rivermist. But she couldn't be the reason Nathan and Neal didn't reconcile, either.

"This isn't about Neal," Nathan responded mutinously, saying his son's name for the first time. "I'm offering to take the heat from that girl's hostile parents for a while, nothing more."

"Bob and Betty are worried sick," Jenn corrected, glancing at Traci. "They're not hostile."

"Oh, they will be, once you move their little princess in here. But—"

"You want to see hostile? You put me in a position where I'm coming between you and your son again, then we'll talk hostile!"

"I'll only add to your distractions around here," Neal cautioned. "And I don't just mean because of Jeremy."

He was talking about their kiss outside, and the ones back at the church, and the instant connection that sparked every time they were together, just like old times. Distance *would* be less distracting, less confusing, but his relationship with his father was more important.

"We'll stay out of each other's way," she insisted. She could do this. "This is a huge house. When I'm not with Traci or Mandy, there's tons to be done around here. And I'm sure you can find something to occupy your time." She made a point of including Nathan in her stare. "It's the best solution for everybody."

It would be impossible. But she'd managed the impossible before. Just look at how amazing her daughter had turned out. A child with no father, raised by the child Jenn had been when she had her. It would be impossible, not falling back in love with Neal, even though he'd be leaving again once Nathan no longer needed him. But she'd handle it.

"Whatever!" More color had leaked from Nathan's complexion in just the last five minutes. "Everybody can stay. Hell—" he headed for the stairs "—why not rent out the extra rooms while you're at it? The more the merrier here at Shangri-La."

THE BLUES. Nathan was lost in the blues as he listened to album after album in the tomblike quietness that had temporarily returned to his house. His boy had stayed the night. Had spent most of the morning on his cell phone and laptop working on some case with a lawyer calling from Atlanta. But he was out jogging now. Had been gone for over an hour. And Jenn and the girls hadn't made it back yet with their things from her father's.

As hard as it was to believe, by tonight there would be four other people living in this house. The thought was nearly as shocking as the thick layer of dust and grime he'd found coating the turntable and album covers. Alone had been his life for so long, the fact that silence felt strange after the last few days wasn't sitting well. Neither was the neglect of what had once been one of the greatest pleasures in his life.

He fingered the age-worn corner of Wanda's favorite Billie Holiday album. Slow and smooth, the magic of the singer's voice had filled nights of slow dancing in this very room. Beautiful, priceless nights with his wife. The memories and the music inter-twined now, bringing with them the beginnings of an honest-to-God smile he was glad no one was there to see. Warm summer Saturdays, long after his wife's death, had been spent listening to Billy and Miles and the countless other artists they'd collected over the years. He'd even brainwashed Neal into liking the *ancient* music, as the kid had called it. Same as he'd passed on his love for broken-down vintage cars and the backbreaking work it took to restore them. Traditions and memories were the center of family, he'd once preached.

Of course, that had been before he'd set his sights on abandoning everyone and everything that had centered him.

"You were going to let me borrow that album, re-member?" a quiet voice asked from the den's doorway.

Nathan ripped the needle off the LP, removed it from the turntable and thrust it and the dusty jacket cover at Joshua Gardner.

"Take it." He squared off against his former best friend. "Got no use for it anymore."

Got no use for any of it.

Jenn's father hesitated, then took the album. It was strangely normal to see him standing there, as he had so many times before. Only the last eight years were reflected in his sad frown and the pity clouding his expression. Exactly the kind of look

Nathan had started locking his doors to keep out. Speaking of which—

"How the hell did you get in here?" He'd locked up behind Jenn when she left, shutting the world out just once more.

The good preacher winced as he held up the spare key they'd exchanged before their kids were born.

"I can't believe you didn't throw that thing away years ago," Nathan grumbled, more surprised than annoyed.

"I can't believe it's taken me this long to use it."

Nathan couldn't deal with Joshua Gardner's sigh of guilt, any more than he'd been able to stomach waking that morning with his son sleeping under his roof for the first time in eight years.

"What, your girl had the balls to come over here first, get the goods on me, so now it's time to barge in at the bitter end to save my soul?"

"No." Jenn got that same *knock it off* look on her face when he went out of his way to be disagreeable. Joshua set the record aside and sat on the sofa. "Your soul was saved a long time before Olivia and I moved to town. I don't figure running everyone off and making a general ass of yourself is going to change whether God wants you or not."

Nathan couldn't help but chuckle. "If you've come here to put me in my place, trust me, your little girl already beat you to it."

The same little girl he'd once blamed, along with her father and the rest of the world, for everything he'd lost. The one now moving in with him with two children in tow. Because she needed to, and he couldn't say no to her if he tried.

"I came to say I'm sorry," Joshua said to the floor. "Things were so messed up, and we both were drowning…making the same mistakes. Beating away at each other didn't fix things, but maybe it was easier…. I don't know. But whatever the excuse, I knew better, and I shouldn't have let it happen. I shouldn't have let you—"

"Let me!" Because the room had begun to tilt, because his head had chosen that moment to begin a new rumba, he dropped into the club chair beside the fireplace. Being dizzy and having a tantrum didn't mix. "Let me what? Walk away from the community you still hold such stock in? Some community, when they still go out of their way to make someone as amazing as your daughter feel unwelcome, just because she sees the world differently. Don't think I don't hear the talk. I know what people are saying. What you don't stop them from saying. And now they're turning on her for helping a messed-up teenager."

Joshua was nodding, but to what exactly was anyone's guess.

"I let you think I didn't care what you were going through," he finally said, emotion roughing up his voice the way it had years ago when he'd dug into one of his better sermons. "Just like I let Jennifer think I didn't want to understand. That I didn't want to make it better somehow. Regardless of what I thought was right or wrong, I owed you both better than that, and I wanted to say I'm sorry."

Sorry was the last word Nathan had expected to hear from anyone in this town. Coming from the last person he'd ever expected to hear from again, period.

"You gonna help that girl of yours?" he demanded.

"As much as she'll let me." Joshua was looking sorrier by the second. "As long as I'm in a position to do her some good."

"Didn't sound like things went too good at the church yesterday."

"No." Joshua shot him a rueful smile. "People are talking a lot more than they're listening. I'm not sure I'm doing much good as their pastor right now. You know how that goes."

And Nathan did.

It was odd how easy it was now to remember what the church and the community were like. Since this man's daughter had barged back into his life, most of the memories weren't so bad anymore.

"Well, who said pastors were supposed to be perfect?" he demanded. "You do right by your child, and that's the best anyone can expect from you."

Joshua nodded. Neither one of them were going to win father of the century.

"Thank you," Joshua said. "For helping Jenn when I couldn't."

"She's done more than that for me." Nathan shrugged off the compliment and a rush of pride at earning his friend's gratitude.

What did he have to be proud of?

"Who would have thought the two of us would end up in exactly the same place," he said, putting words to the hateful reality of just how many mistakes they had in common. "Me, an alcoholic bum looking for every chance I can get to make the end come a little quicker. And you, a by-the-book preacher who played by the rules and expected that to save him. Meanwhile we both managed to lose our kids."

It was Nathan's old friend who looked up from the floor then. Not Pastor Gardner, but the good man who'd once shared every secret Nathan had.

"I just pray it's not too late to get them back," Joshua said. "I'd give anything to make things work here for Jenn this time."

"And I'd give anything to make Neal leave," Nathan replied, needing his friend in that moment. Needing to say it to someone. "Before he finds out just how much I want him to stay."

CHAPTER FIFTEEN

THE BANGING WOKE NEAL out of a deep sleep. Deeper sleep than he'd ever remembered having. So deep, for a minute he had no idea where he was. Just the vague longing to make the noise stop so he could go on sleeping.

The next crash had other ideas.

He jerked awake to find himself sitting in his childhood bed, in a room overflowing with memories his father had held on to, the sheet twisted around his naked body. Sleeping naked was another post-prison luxury, one that came along with privacy and closed doors that people couldn't see through.

A louder crash had him reaching for his jeans, thoughts of Jeremy Compton's angry face and threats from last night propelling him out of the room and down the stairs. The ruckus was definitely coming from out back. Jenn and her daughter and Traci had moved in that afternoon, and he'd be damned if he'd let Jeremy keep making trouble for them.

He'd almost reached the kitchen door to the

backyard when a shadow by the sink moved. Turning, he found himself face-to-face with the amazing sight of Jennifer Gardner in her nightshirt, standing in the puddle of moonlight streaming through the window.

And then it was as if he were still dreaming. As if walking toward her, taking her hand and laying it on his bare chest, over his heart, was the answer to eight years of feeling nothing. Just this once, just in this dream, he wouldn't be alone anymore. In this moment, he could feel again, and the emotions wouldn't destroy him.

There were tears in her eyes. He kissed them away, but more followed. Tears that broke his heart.

"Don't be afraid, Jennifer," he said. In his dreams, he could call her Jennifer. "Let me make you happy. We don't have to be alone anymore."

She shook her head.

"It's too late," she whispered. "It's—"

His mouth covered the words that would break the spell, wanting this dream to be about what they both needed, rather than what they wouldn't let themselves have.

Her hands came up to cup his face as his covered her breasts. Her soft moan, the fingers now tugging at his hair, tugging his mouth closer as their tongues began to dance, shot him to the edge of release— from just kissing her. And because it was a dream, he didn't make himself stop. He pushed her against the counter instead. Let his hand roam down her side to her hip, and then around to the sweet feel of her bottom. Sweetness he'd once kissed every inch of and thought he'd have forever to memorize.

An enormous crash and the sound of glass breaking jerked them apart. Jenn strained against the counter beside the sink, the moon still shrouding her in dreamlike mystery, while he stumbled away until he bumped against the refrigerator, reality returning with a rush.

She still needed him; there was no way she could deny it now. But her wrecked expression said it all. There was also no way she could let herself have what the last few minutes promised.

It's too late.

She needed to be free of the past too badly. And as he'd promised himself earlier, he couldn't do anything but give her what she needed. He owed her at least that.

Crash!

He stalked toward the back door, sexual frustration and regret fueling the need to stomp Jeremy Compton into the ground.

"Neal, no!" Jenn grabbed his arm. "It... It's Nathan. He's in the garage."

Her tears were back, this time for his father, whom she was strong enough to help even though it meant watching the man die. Compassion and strength. Amazing gifts in anyone, but especially someone who'd been through all she had. He'd shut down completely. He'd run from feeling anything. But her ability to love and protect had grown even stronger— even if she was caring for everyone but herself.

"Go back to bed," he said, brushing a chaste kiss across the lips he wanted to still be devouring. "I'll take care of him."

And when he stepped into the yard and headed toward the clanging mess his father was making in the garage they'd once worked side by side in, he knew this time there'd be no running. This time, because it was important to Jenn—and because of her, important to him now, too—he and his...*dad*...were going to face each other and the past they'd both been running from for too long.

NATHAN LIFTED the wooden mallet and took another swing at the vintage car he'd wasted years restoring. So many years of waiting, of not giving up hope that one day Neal would walk through the door, pick up a wrench and start helping him. Give the boy time, he'd reasoned. One day, Neal would be there and want this hunk of junk as much as he did. Want to fight for their relationship, even though Nathan didn't deserve that kind of loyalty from the son he'd adandoned.

Wham! He broke through the passenger window

he'd custom ordered from some body shop in Macon. *Wham!* He kept beating away at it, the way he should have two years ago when he'd finally finished the thing and Neal still hadn't come back. When it had become clear he was never coming. That Nathan had gotten what he'd said he'd wanted. He was totally alone.

Wham! Only the boy was here now. *Wham!* Now that there was no time for anything but goodbye.

Why the hell had he kept this damn thing? That was the question. Polishing it. Hiding it away. Keeping it in top running condition while everything else in his world rotted away.

"Dad," a quiet voice said from the door. "Dad? Are you all right?"

Nathan wielded the mallet at his boy.

Was he all right?

"What are you doing?" Neal asked, wincing as he surveyed the destruction Nathan had achieved in the last half hour.

Just about anyone else could have accomplished more. But his throbbing head made every slam against the car excruciating—exactly the way he'd wanted it.

"I'm settling my estate," he quipped, the mallet breaking off the rearview mirror this time, the momentum of the swing pitching him sideways. The tool slipped from his hand. He braced himself against his worktable—a table filled with tools he'd never use again. "Downsizing. Getting rid of crap so I don't have to deal with it anymore. So no one else has to deal with it later."

"I can't believe you finished this car." His son ran a reverent hand over the paint job Nathan had left several not-big-enough-to-be-satisfying dents in.

Letting the worktable take more of his weight so he could catch his breath, Nathan snorted. "Neither can I."

"I never thought I'd see this place again." The man his boy had become looked around him, memories of countless hours they'd tinkered out here together playing across his face.

"Neither did I," Nathan responded carefully.

"If…" Neal took a step closer. "If I'd known you needed help…I'd have come back sooner…. I've been working on my own hunk of scrap for three years now."

Nathan nodded.

I'd have come back sooner.

"Yeah, I saw your ride in the driveway. Looks like you've done a fine job with it."

The kind of job any father would be proud of.

"I never forgot about this one, though." His boy stooped and glanced inside at the vintage leather seats Nathan had bought off the Internet, from a junk dealer in Alaska, of all places. He straightened back up.

"I…I just thought it was better that I stayed put in Atlanta. I thought you were doing fine on your own, so…"

"I don't want to talk about this." Nathan reached down for the mallet. The floor was suddenly rushing toward him.

Neal caught his arm and helped him back to the workbench.

"Well, I *do* want to talk about it," his boy said. "If we don't talk about it now, then when?"

"How about never!" Nathan managed to grab the mallet. Pushing to his feet, he took aim for the right front quarter panel. "Sometimes it's just too late. Some things can't be saved."

Neal stopped his swing with ridiculously little effort and took the mallet away.

"You can beat away at this thing all you want, Dad, but it's not going to disappear. And neither am I. I know you don't want me here—"

"Don't want you here!" Nathan jerked away from his grasp, then shoved his son back several feet. "I want this damn car. I want you. I want it all so badly I can't stand to look at either one of you anymore!"

"Dad—"

"Damn it, get out!" He shoved again, only this time the kid was ready and he didn't move an inch. "Get out! Take your car and the life you've built.

You deserve to be happy. I don't want you here watching…"

"Watching you die?"

Nathan turned and swept every tool off the workbench.

"Do you have any idea," he rasped, "what it's like to look at what you'd give anything to keep? Only it's all slipping away right before your eyes, and there's nothing you can do to stop it? Don't you see? If you're not here…"

The silence between them went on so long, Nathan finally turned back to his son.

"If I'm not here, then there's nothing to lose?" his boy asked.

"Yeah," was all Nathan could manage.

Neal nodded, staring down at the mallet he'd confiscated. "Prison was like that. As long as I had nothing, no one, it was okay. But remembering…seeing you every month when you came to visit. It was like dying every time you left. Being trapped in something like that can make a man want to destroy what he cares the most about."

The understanding in his boy's words, the perfect picture he'd painted of the ugliness raging through Nathan, reached out like a benediction. A bridge to the kind of understanding that shouldn't be possible between them. Not after all this time.

"Yeah," Nathan agreed again, finding a monkey

wrench and testing its weight in his hand. "Like maybe destroying it will make you stop wanting it so much."

He took a swing at the back fender. The impact shot pain through his skull at the same time that the wrench dented the lovingly hand-buffed chrome.

"It doesn't work, you know," his son said between his teeth as he wielded the mallet against the windshield, shattering it and sending shards of vintage glass everywhere. "Making what you want the most go away… In the long run, it only ends up making you want it even more."

"Then I guess it's my lucky day." Nathan took aim at the roof, grinning at his boy as he did. "'Cause I ain't got no long run to worry about anymore."

CHAPTER SIXTEEN

"MOMMY, ARE NATHAN and Neal making up?" Mandy asked Jenn while they took out garbage.

Traci had tried to make her first lasagna tonight, with questionable results. Which meant there were more scraps in the trash than there were leftovers in the fridge.

"They're trying, honey." Father and son had finally talked. They'd destroyed half the garage and Nathan's remodeled car, but in the days since, there had been a lessening of tension between them, giving Jenn hope that their relationship was mending.

Neal had made a point of avoiding her since that night. Since their heartbreaking kiss in the kitchen. He worked over the phone or on his laptop, picked odd jobs around the house that he could do by himself or was off running for hours on end. Often running late at night because it seemed he wasn't having any easier time sleeping than she was. He kept busy and kept out of her way. Exactly what she'd needed him to do.

He and Nathan were together inside, playing a quiet game of Monopoly while Nathan's favorite Miles Davis album filled the den with jazz. The old man still glared at Neal every few minutes, as if he hated his son for being exactly where he needed him. They bickered over nonsense, what little they did speak. But Nathan was no longer telling Neal to leave. She'd even seen him smile at his son's back more than once as Neal walked away. She'd seen light begin to shine in those old, dark eyes again.

Maybe they'd said everything they needed to the other night. Or maybe they'd agreed to avoid what needed to be said most of all. Either way, Nathan was being cared for—*knew* he was cared for—and that's what mattered. Things were going so well in fact, if it weren't for Traci still needing someplace to crash, Jenn would have quietly slipped away days ago.

From both the Cain men.

"So Neal came home to help his daddy?" Mandy asked. "The way you did Grandpa?"

"Sort of."

Mandy hadn't wanted to move away from her Grandpa's—a fact that had both charmed and alarmed Jenn's father the morning he'd helped them pack to come here. Then Jenn had explained that Mr. Cain was still sick and needed a lot of help. After that, her little trouper had signed on, ready to do her part.

Ready to help her friend.

She threw both her and Mandy's trash bags into the container at the curb. "Honey, you know how Grandpa's getting better now?"

"Yeah, he was grumpy, too, when we first moved in. But the better he got the nicer he got." The world's most beautiful smile told Jenn just how much this child had fallen in love with the grandfather she would never have known if they hadn't moved home to Rivermist. "That's why I don't mind Grandpa Nathan's grumpy face so much. I know it'll get better, just like my real grandpa's did. I know he likes me, anyway."

"Of course he likes you." It had taken the child's little finger less time to snag Nathan than it had Jenn's dad. "But, honey, not everyone gets better like Grandpa. Sometimes the people we help get worse, no matter what we do."

"Is Mr. Cain getting worse?" Mandy's forehead wrinkled with worry. "That doesn't mean we're going to stop helping, does it?"

"No, we're not going to stop helping." Jenn knelt until they were eye-to-eye. "We're going to stay for as long as Traci and Mr. Cain need us to. As long as that's okay with you. Grandpa's offered to let you stay with him while I'm here with Traci, if you want to go back."

"But I want to stay," Mandy insisted. "You get to help people all the time. It's my turn."

Jenn pulled her daughter into her arms. Held tight to the new beginning Mandy had found in Rivermist. A grandfather she hadn't known before. New friends, and a growing desire to help other people, either through activities at her grandfather's church or living with a grumpy old man, she didn't seem to care which.

This was what Jenn had longed for when she'd decided to give this home of her childhood a chance to be more than somewhere she dreaded. She cuddled her child's sweet-smelling body close, her miracle second chance that rivaled anything she could have dreamed of when she'd left. Even when Nathan and Traci no longer needed her, even when she had to leave this house and Neal behind, she'd have Mandy's new beginning to hold on to.

Neal.

Don't be afraid, Jennifer. Let me make you happy. We don't have to be alone anymore.

How had he known she still felt alone, even back in this town with people who'd known her since she was a baby?

Helping other people, taking care of them, was her life. A life that satisfied her on so many levels. But happy? Just the thought of trying for happy again, trying with Neal, had kept her from tracking him down in this monstrous place for days. Kept her from trying to explain how much his kisses had meant, and why they terrified her.

Hugging Mandy a little tighter, she looked through the chilly night at the Cain house, thinking of the happiness that had once ruled there. The joy that was creeping back into Nathan's life now, because he wasn't alone anymore. He had Neal back.

Joy she didn't know how to grab hold of for herself and not need to shove away just as quickly.

Had it really been so long since she'd been truly happy, that she was actually afraid to want it anymore?

"HEY, TRACI." Brett Hamilton slipped around the corner and caught Traci hiding behind her locker door. "Got a second?"

Oh, no.

No, no, no, no, no.

Mortified, even more than when she'd seen him at the church council meeting, Traci slammed her locker door and made a beeline for first period honors calculus. Please let Brett take the hint, be the good guy he'd always been before and leave her to wallow in her mess.

There was no point in saying she was sorry. Cheating on the town's favorite Boy Scout, so she could move on to being knocked up by a loser, wasn't something you could *sorry* away. *Let's be friends* made even less sense. She'd given up on her friends, mostly because they'd given up on her. Even Shelly had gone out of her way to be too busy talking with another girl that morning to say hi. Traci was quickly becoming damaged goods that no one would be seen with.

At least it was Friday, and she'd have the weekend to hide away and bury herself in cleaning up the old Cain house some more.

"Traci." Brett caught up, even though his English class was on the other side of the building. "I need to talk with you."

She stopped at that.

No one *needed* to talk with her anymore. For sure not her rule-freak parents who still hadn't visited her at the Cain place.

"I wanted to…" Brett steered her toward the stairwell. Everyone else was in class or trying to get there before the late bell, leaving the normally busy alcove empty but still smelling like sweaty socks. "I wanted to ask, you know, if you and the baby were okay?"

Okay?

Was he kidding?

Was she really supposed to stand there looking at Brett, the boy who'd worshiped her since kindergarten, and talk about the baby she'd basically punked him to make with another guy?

Had her choices really dwindled to either humiliating herself, or taking the calculus test she hadn't studied for last night?

"Everyone's talking about you moving over to the Cain house," he added.

Differential equations, here she came.

Brett blocked her escape, something he'd never done before. In fact, part of the reason she'd started looking at other guys was to see if Brett would ever work up the nerve to try and stop her.

"I haven't been listening to any of the gossip," he assured her. "Especially all that shit Jeremy Compton's saying about Neal Cain, and how dangerous he is, and how he and Jenn are getting it on again now that you're all living at his dad's place."

Brett blushed.

Traci smiled before she had time to remember that she no longer had any right to get mushy over how cute he was.

"Okay," he amended. "I've listened to some of it. But only because I'm worried you're getting yourself into more trouble. I didn't want to butt in, but I thought maybe if you wanted to talk… You know, maybe I could help if you needed something."

She blinked.

He was actually giving her the chance to speak for herself? He was worried?

"You really are a nice guy, Brett."

He shrugged her words away. "So are things okay? Over there I mean. Is Neal Cain—"

"Neal's fine, I guess. I mean, I don't know what

goes on during the day while I'm here. But he and Jenn are working on the house all the time. Or he's playing some stupid game with Mr. Cain. They keep arguing over which lousy old record to play. Nobody talks to me much but Jenn and Mandy, and the kid's—"

"How about you?" More blushing. "You and the baby. Are things getting any better, you know, with your parents?"

Before she'd lost her mind with *the jackass,* Brett had listened to all her crap about her parents. Really listened. He'd actually been interested, not just trying to get into her pants.

And she'd tossed him away.

"You know what Bob and Betty are like," she said. "Nothing's going to be okay unless they have their way. And that's not going to happen this time. I can't go back home if they won't even talk to me. What kind of life would that be for my baby, seeing how Grandma and Grandpa are so totally sure Mommy's not capable of doing anything on her own? I'm nobody's dream-mom, but I know enough not to warp a kid from the cradle like that."

Brett's blue, blue eyes actually smiled.

"You're doing the right thing," he said. "A lot of us think so."

"A lot of who?" He didn't mean it. He couldn't, not after—

"A lot of the kids. What you and Ms. Gardner are doing, making this about your choices instead of just about what your folks want, it's great."

Great?

"I cheated on you, Brett."

"Yeah." His smile vanished. His eyes filled with shadows she'd never seen before. "Why didn't you just tell me you wanted us over? Why all the cloak-and-dagger shit, just to make me look stupid?"

"I don't know why I did any of it."

Except she did. Hours of talking with Jenn while they worked around the Cain house the last couple of days—spending hours at night by herself, since her parents and the *friends* who thought she was doing the right thing had conveniently forgotten to come around—had helped her figure out more than she'd ever wanted to know about the shallow, selfish things she'd done. She hadn't wanted things over with Brett, as much as she'd been trying to prove to herself that being with him wasn't all she was. That what her parents expected wasn't all she'd ever be.

Never once had she stopped to think that she didn't have the first clue who she wanted to be herself. The hot single chick with the older guy thing had certainly been a bust. And hiding out at the Cain place waiting for everything to magically work out on its own hadn't been going much better.

"I'm not sure I know anything anymore." Looking

at Brett's confused frown, the strength in his mile-wide shoulders, made her want to throw her arms around him and beg him to take her back. To make everything okay by loving her again. Like that was going to happen. "But I'm learning, thanks to Jenn. She's the one who's great."

"You don't seem to be doing so badly." It was a reluctant smile this time, but the fact that he could still smile at her at all had the mushy stuff inside turning even mushier. "I can't see Shelly Ackerson or the rest of the crew buckling down and going the full ten rounds with their parents. You're tougher than you think, Carpenter."

He gave her a guy's nudge to the shoulder that felt better than a thousand hugs.

"But if you need anything in that crazy place you're living in, I want you to…" He ducked his head. "You know… Call me. No matter what's happened, I want you to be okay. You and your baby both."

He was jogging away before she could say anything else. Running from what he'd said, and from the tears streaming down her face.

It was a bunch of crap, him saying she was stronger than her friends. That she was up for this ridiculous stand she'd taken. She'd felt strong for, like, a minute when she stood up to her parents at that meeting. Now, days of puking up her breakfast later, she was back to wanting to run like the scared little girl she still was.

You're stronger than you think.

Maybe Brett could clue her parents in, if he was so sure!

All Bob and Betty saw when they looked at her was their baby girl, and their biggest disappointment.

The darkness of the empty stairwell closed in around her. The sound of another girl's laughter filtered down from one of the floors above. Someone else's happiness echoing just how alone she really was.

Stop being such a baby!

She had Jenn in her corner, and even sick old Mr. Cain. And hadn't Brett just offered to help if she needed him. An offer of unspoken forgiveness she so didn't deserve.

Giving up, wasting even a second feeling sorry for herself would let everyone down, her baby most of all. The tiny life that just yesterday the clinic doctor had said was perfectly healthy as she did an ultrasound. The life growing deep inside her that she couldn't believe she'd ever considered ending.

No matter how easy it would be, giving up wasn't an option. And she was tired of waiting for her parents to come to her, too. If she was so strong, what was she waiting for? After school, she was heading to her parents' house and inviting them to dinner. Something Jenn had been on her case to do since the church council meeting. Tomorrow was her night to cook, and she and Jenn had already planned the menu—one more thing she could do now that she'd never even thought about just weeks ago.

Things with her parents were going to work out or they weren't. But thanks to Jenn, she knew she was going to be okay, even if it meant being by herself.

THE SOUND OF CHIRPING filtered through Neal's apartment window. He growled and buried his head farther beneath the feather pillows he'd spent a fortune on because he'd slept on them as a kid. There must be a new family of birds nesting in the tree outside. The one his landlord wouldn't cut down.

The high-pitched, happy tune continued, taking him back to where he never went anymore—to the lazy summer mornings of his childhood. Half dreaming, half awake, he let himself remember days filled with nothing important stretched out before him, an open invitation to run free. School was out for the summer and life was good. He could do anything he wanted.

Sunlight warmed his closed lids, tempting him to wake. He never slept this late. He was usually in the office before sunup. But this morning he couldn't move. He rolled away as he had several times already, no longer fighting the pull of remembering. Letting the dreams come.

Then the sound of giggling joined the bird's noise. Followed by the oddest sensation along his right side. He jerked and was rewarded with another giggle. Lifting an eyelid, he saw a hand snake along the mattress, headed toward his side again.

In an instant, prison instincts took over. He grabbed the hand, yanked whoever it was against the bed as hard as his awkward position would allow, and was rewarded with an ear-piercing scream. Jack-knifing more fully awake, he rubbed his eyes and tried to focus on the impossible appearance of a life-sized Tweety Bird floating beside his bed.

"What the—" He winced as the next scream split his head in two.

"Mandy!" The door banged open.

Then time stood still as Jennifer Gardner flew into the room, gasping at the sight of Neal holding her squirming daughter by the arm.

The world righted itself. Visions from childhood and prison dissolved into the here and now. Fight-or-flight instincts receded, leaving behind the sharp tang of adrenaline coating his tongue.

He was on the outside now. He was safe.

More to the point, he wasn't in his apartment in Atlanta sleeping a work morning away. It was a

Rivermist Saturday, he was in his old room and he'd just scared Jennifer Gardner's daughter half to death.

His heartbeat settling, he scrambled to secure the sheet at his hip as Jenn dropped to her knees beside the little girl and pulled her close. Mandy buried her head in the golden hair cascading down her mother's neck.

"She startled me." He rubbed a hand across his face. "I didn't know who it was. She—"

"She was tickling you," Jennifer explained.

"What?"

"Tickling you." Jennifer's expression softened into a lopsided grin that had the unfortunate effect of waking a very morning-conscious part of his anatomy. "That's how she wakes her grandfather before she leaves for school, isn't it, sweetie?"

She jostled Mandy, kissing the little girl's neck and nudging her chin. "It's okay, honey. Neal doesn't know how to play your game. He didn't mean to scare you." Then she looked at him, worry and understanding crowding out the fake cheerfulness she'd used with her daughter. "I'm sorry she woke you. I was trying to get out of here quietly, hoping you were finally getting some sleep."

He'd been up half the night playing board games with his dad. They played more and more every day. Nathan tired too easily now for his favorite pastime: tinkering in the garage. But they were spending time together, his dad's anger softening. The real man beneath reluctantly emerging to find some peace in hanging out with his son late at night when the rest of the world was asleep. Same as when Neal had been a kid.

All thanks to the beautiful woman kneeling next to his bed, close for the first time since their last kiss.

Jennifer.

"Jenn" was impossible now.

Her gaze slipped to the sheet covering his very bare lap. Her cheeks flushed, the way they had when he'd kissed her in the kitchen, and wanted to keep kissing her…. He'd wanted to lay her out on the table, strip off her nightgown and forget the reality crashing down on top of both of them.

But she'd been crying… Wanting him made her cry.

"Um…" he mumbled.

"We're heading out." She wobbled to her feet, lifting Mandy with her.

"I'm sorry," he said again. "I didn't mean to—"

"I know." She smiled over her shoulder, the simple beauty of it killing him. "We're heading out with Traci to do some grocery shopping."

The door shut as she backed completely out of the room, then he was alone. Alone with ghosts from the childhood he hadn't let himself remember before moving back here.

The bird outside kept up its nattering, echoing the past that kept rushing back the longer he stayed in this place. Planting the seed of a killer headache directly behind his right eye. An ache that had come and gone a dozen times since helping his dad dismantle the vintage car the man had slaved over. Not more than a few words had been exchanged as they'd reduced the Mustang to scrap once more. Silently bashing away at what they should have built together.

Neal picked up his watch, checked the time and slipped it onto his wrist. It was nine o'clock, when he'd planned to be up at dawn doing something— anything he could get his hands on—as he waited for whatever was supposed to happen next between him and his dad.

His dad.

They hadn't come close to talking about anything real yet. Nothing close to goodbye or…or saying they loved each other just one more time.

Maybe his dad would never be ready for that.

Neal grunted.

Or maybe *he* was still too chickenshit.

Do you have any idea what it's like…?

And he did. He understood the prison his father had built for himself all too well. And whether they said another damn word to each other or not, whether he spent every night either jogging or staring sleepless at the ceiling, he was going to be here. He was going to make sure loneliness didn't add to his father's burdens.

But the drive inside him continued to churn. The need to run. Not from Nathan anymore, but from the woman living with them whose silence and loneliness were even harder to stomach.

Jenn worked furiously around the house, taught the Carpenter girl how to cook and clean when Traci wasn't in school. Basically spent her time hiding from the town she'd not so long ago hoped to make a fresh start in. The rumors about the two of them had been steadily growing according to Reverend Gardner—compliments of a still-pissed-off Jeremy Compton.

But Jenn had stayed, regardless, even if she'd stayed well out of Neal's way.

He reached for the box he'd placed under his bed. The shoebox holding Jenn's unopened letters. Letters that screamed how much he was a part of her reasons for fearing the love and passion still burning inside her. He'd shut her out. Let her down. Left her alone and hurting, and now she was afraid to ever again reach for anything close to what they'd had.

What could he say to make all she'd been through go away?

Don't be afraid, Jennifer…. Let me make you happy. We don't have to be alone anymore.

He'd said it. And he'd been too late.

Feminine laughter filtered up the stairs, bringing with it the sharp memory of Jennifer laughing in his arms at the homecoming dance, smiling. Her eyes shining with forever, as if she never wanted to leave that moment.

Cursing, Neal stalked across the room for his clothes.

Run.

He needed a run.

It took him less than a minute to throw on the sweats that made the temperatures outside bearable, then he bounded down the stairs. He heard someone puttering in the den and headed out the front door and down the silent street. And every step he took brought with it the impulse to turn around. To head back and beg Jennifer not to make him say goodbye to her, too, the way he'd soon have to say goodbye to his dad.

But he'd promised. He wasn't going to hurt her anymore.

So he took the turn at the end of the street and kept on running.

CHAPTER SEVENTEEN

"THEY DID AN ULTRASOUND this week when I went in for my first prenatal visit," Traci said as she poured gravy over her mother's mashed potatoes—instant mashed potatoes that Traci had made herself. But Jenn had beamed proudly as if the teenager made them all by herself.

The Carpenters had actually agreed to dinner at the Cain house. Jenn was still having trouble believing it. Well, Betty had agreed after answering the door yesterday to Traci's *I won't take no for an answer* invitation. Bob had come along for the ride, but that didn't mean the man wanted to be there. But he *was* there, and Traci finally had her chance to talk with her parents one-on-one, without any outside interference.

Nathan had eaten earlier in the den with Mandy. He was falling asleep in front of one Mandy's favorite videos now, and Neal was out for another run. Jenn caught herself checking her watch and wondering when he would be back. The house felt different without him there. Everything felt different, and he was gone more and more often every day.

Knock it off.

Focus on the awkward chitchat.

Chitchat that had just veered into dangerous territory.

Traci had wanted her parents to make the first move. She wasn't going to force them to talk about her pregnancy. But after twenty minutes of strained silence, the girl had cracked.

"Is…" Betty's forkful of butter beans returned to her plate. She glanced at her husband, and then to Jenn, of all people. Anyone but Traci. "Is everything okay with the baby?"

"Everything's fine." Traci cast Jenn a frustrated glance. Jenn gave extra attention to cutting in to her overcooked baked chicken. "In fact, everything's great. They've given me a delivery date. The baby's due late in August."

Jenn watched the Carpenters' reaction from under her lashes, continuing to eat as if this were normal dinner table conversation between a close-knit family. Traci had asked her to stay for moral support, otherwise she'd have joined Nathan for the Disney double-feature in the den.

"That's…" Betty glanced to her husband. "You're birthday's in August, Bob."

"Cool, huh?" Traci pounced on her mother's

feeble show of interest. She seemed to be intentionally not noticing the way her father hadn't eaten a bite the entire meal. The way his hands were now clenched on either side of his plate. "You're going to have the same sign, Dad."

"Cool?" Bob's face turned a nasty shade of red. "Astrological signs? You're having a baby you have no idea how to take care of, and the best you can come up with is, cool?"

"No." Traci swallowed a lump of mashed potatoes. Her wobbly but brave smile met her dad's glare. "The best is that I'm healthy, and so is the baby. I may not know everything I need to yet, but I know I'm going to finish high school, with honors, even if you don't get to throw the world's most perfect graduation party because you'll be too ashamed of your knocked-up daughter to celebrate. And I talked to the school counselor this week about junior colleges. Jenn's helping me learn to cook, and to do laundry, so I can be a good mom, and—"

"Junior college?" Bob dropped his napkin on top of the untouched plate of food Traci had worked hours to prepare. "You wanted to be a journalist last time I checked. Ivy League with your friends was all you'd talk about. How do you propose to get the degree and experience you'll need while you're going to some nowhere college and trying to support a baby on your own?"

"I won't be alone," the teenager countered, reassuring herself while she pushed her dad over the edge. "I'll find the help I need from…from somewhere."

Bob Carpenter pushed back from the table with a shriek of chair legs against hardwood. "What are you going to do for child care, Traci? For money to buy the food you're learning how to cook, or buy the clothes you're suddenly so interested in knowing how to clean? Up till now, your idea of sorting laundry has been tossing your designer duds on the floor and pulling the tags off something from your bottomless closet. A couple of days of home ec with Jenn, and now you're ready to be a mom? Have this baby on your own, and you'll never make it."

Every ugly word came from a place of worry and concern for his daughter. Jenn could see that from his haggard expression and the lines of fatigue bracketing his frown. She doubted the man had slept a night since Traci moved out. But every word had been absolutely the wrong thing to say.

"Actually—" Jenn covered Traci's hand, trying to put as much support as possible into the squeeze she gave the girl's fingers "—Traci's a fast study. I don't think there's anything she can't learn, once she sets her mind to it. She couldn't even boil water a couple of days ago, but she pulled tonight's dinner together herself. All I did was chop a few things here and there and supervise."

Bob scanned the table full of food. All of his favorites. Traci had made sure of it.

Betty gave his arm a tentative pat. "Isn't it wonderful? Everything's so delicious. I don't think I could have done better."

"Jenn's signed me up for parenting and baby-care classes at the clinic in Colter." Traci sat straighter, calm and determined now, where just a week ago she would have chosen rebellion to beat back at her father. "I have a lot to learn. But I can do this. I know that now. I want this baby to have the best I can give—"

"You don't have anything to give it! You're only seventeen. This is your doing." Bob glowered at Jenn. "You just don't know when to quit."

"I—" Jenn began.

"Jenn's encouraged me to move home all along, Daddy. I'm still here in spite of her advice, not because of it. And even though she doesn't always agree with me, she's supporting me instead of telling me what I *can't* do. So are Reverend Gardner and Mr. Cain. You should be thanking them, not pointing fingers."

"Thanking them?" Bob looked ready to scream. "You're my child not theirs, and—"

"I'm not a child anymore!" Traci shouted back.

"Bob—" Betty's hand clenched on her husband's arm.

"No." He pushed out of his chair. "I'm not going to sit here while my daughter tells me I should be thanking the people pandering to her irresponsible fantasies."

"Trust me, Daddy. I'm not living a fantasy!" Traci shot up from her seat, too. "I've been puking into a toilet every morning. I've lost my friends, my family. And by the fall, I'm going to have another life depending on me. Me, Dad! I'm about as responsible as I can get. So don't worry. I get it. I've totally messed up. And if it weren't for Jenn I don't know where I'd be right now, but you can bet it sure wouldn't be here in Rivermist. So maybe you *should* be angry with her. It's her fault I'm not out of your hair and off messing up somewhere else where you don't have to watch."

"We don't want you anywhere else." Betty reached for her daughter, as if desperate to hold on, in case the teen ran that very second. "We want you to come home."

"No." Traci moved away. "I can't. Not if going home means spending the rest of my pregnancy being told day after day that this baby is a mistake. That I should be ashamed, and be sorry, and that I can't do this. My child's future depends on me, and I'll never make it if all I hear is how young and weak and stupid I am. Here with Jenn, or somewhere else where there are centers where girls like me can start over, at least I'll have people who support me. Total strangers who'll at least lie to me and tell me I can do this, so I don't just curl up in a corner somewhere and quit."

"Honey, we want to support you." Betty's eyes filled with tears. She turned to her husband. "Tell her, Bob. Tell her we want her to stay in Rivermist, to come home. That we'll do whatever it takes to make this work."

"Of course we don't want you to leave." Bob's chin wobbled.

The first encouraging sign Jenn had seen.

She peeked in Traci's direction to find the teenager blinking valiantly at her own tears.

"But you don't want me home, do you? Not *me*." A single tear fell. Traci wiped it away. "You want your little girl back. Your perfect high school graduate with a college scholarship and a prom to plan. You don't want *me*, messed-up and making you crazy. I want things you don't want. Things you don't approve of, and you can't deal with that."

"We want you safe." Bob cleared his throat. "We want your baby safe. We'll do whatever we have to do to make that happen."

Traci cocked her head to the side, pondering her father's pseudoconcession. Jenn held her breath.

Reached for the faith her father had once helped her believe could breathe life into unsteady hope, until it was strong enough to fly on its own.

She wanted this so much for Traci. *For Traci,* she reminded herself. This family's success and failure had nothing to do with Jenn or whatever happiness she managed to find in her life.

Her father was right. So was her boss back in North Carolina. She became too attached to the lives of the people she helped. Identified too much with their ups and downs, rather than riding her own roller-coaster. She wasn't going to do that this time. Not to Traci.

"This isn't just my baby, Daddy." The teenager covered her still-flat tummy and smiled. "This is my child. Your *grandchild.* Being safe isn't enough. I want this baby to be loved."

"Traci," Betty said. "We love you. Please, come home."

But Traci wouldn't look away from her father. A man who couldn't seem to say another word. Shaking her head, she grabbed her plate and silverware and headed for the kitchen. When Betty stood to follow, Jenn reached for the woman's arm.

"Give her some time, Mrs. Carpenter."

"Don't tell us what to do with our child." Bob pulled his wife against his side. "This entire situation never would have happened if you'd done your job and let us do ours."

"You know—" Jenn picked up the bowls of potatoes and beans "—your first step might be to stop blaming your daughter, and me, and whoever else is convenient at the time for what's happened. All blame accomplishes is pushing people away. Traci made a mistake. She accepts that. Why can't you?"

"We have accepted it." His eyes hardened. "We've asked her to move home. But it seems you've still won, haven't you? She'd rather be here than with us."

"This has nothing to do with me." Jenn worked hard to believe that.

The girl's family situation was so much like the one she had lost, it wasn't easy. The realization that Traci was stronger than Jenn had been at her age, that the girl had the grit to keep reaching for the kind of happiness Jenn had finally stopped believing in all together, made it even harder.

"The only people who are going to lose if you can't accept your daughter the way she is," she continued, "are you and your wife. I have no doubt that Traci's going to come out of this just fine. She's an amazing young woman, and she and her baby are going to have an amazing life not only full of hard work and obstacles, but full of joy and hope, too. You can either be a part of that, or not."

She headed for the kitchen before she said anything else. Before more of what she wanted, what she'd never had, touched this situation that wasn't about her at all. The room was empty, the back door ajar. Through the window above the sink, Jenn caught a flash of Traci's sweatshirt—the girl was standing beside Jenn's car.

Her shoulders shook with emotion as Jenn approached. From around front came the slam of car doors shutting. An engine firing. Traci flinched as she listened to her parents driving away.

"They're never going to forget what I said in there," she cried. "I can't believe I talked to my dad like that."

"Never is a long time, sweetie. You were sure Brett would never talk to you again." Jenn hugged her, rocking slowly as she did when she was soothing Mandy. "Didn't you say he offered to help you if you needed it?"

"That's different." She shrugged off Jenn's embrace. "That…that's friendship. My parents are all about control. What I think. What I feel. What I do. They're never going to change. They think this baby is something to be ashamed of, because they're ashamed of me. It's their grandchild, and they can't be happy about it. This is never going to work! I might as well…I…I need to get out of here."

Jenn stilled at the teen's words. Get out of the

house for a while, or out of town? She couldn't let that happen! She wouldn't accept another—

Accept?

She closed her eyes against the echoes of her own past. Traci's choices weren't hers to accept or change. This wasn't about her life, her happiness. No matter how much she wanted to go back and find a way to keep believing in the future, the way Traci had up until this moment. The way Jenn had to believe the teenager still would once she had a chance to calm down.

Help the girl, Jenn. Focus on the girl!

Focusing on someone else. Jenn's specialty.

"Go ahead," she said, digging her keys from her jeans pocket. "Take my car if you need to go for a drive. While you're gone, I'll…" *Get my head out of my ass and get my priorities straight?* "I'll take care of the dishes."

Jenn watched the teen drive slowly away, her heart breaking at the sight of Traci's tears. The girl still had a chance, a chance she'd given herself by staying in Rivermist through all this confusion instead of running. A chance that circumstances and loss and too much grief had stolen from Jenn. Traci would find another way. Jenn had to believe that.

She walked back toward the broken-down house that had become a home again. Thought of the men who lived there together now, even if only temporarily. Thought of all the reasons she'd returned to Rivermist and stayed—for Mandy, for her father, and then for Nathan and Traci. Her hope had been that they would all find their way before it was too late.

God, please don't let it be too late, she pleaded.

But for the first time she wasn't thinking of the other lives she'd spent so much time and energy helping. As she sat at the picnic table where Neal had kissed her for the second time since coming home— coming home to both his father and her—she realized she was pleading for herself.

Neal wanted to love her. To find a way to be happy again…with her.

Lord, how she wanted that, too. Only she was too scared to even try.

The people she cared so much about were responsible for their own happiness. Her training told her that. But them having their happiness to find meant leaving her to search for her own.

Watching Traci fight for her and her child's future left Jenn shaken. Maybe even made her a little jealous.

What about *her* life? The happiness she'd never stopped to fight for, because there'd always been something else, someone else, that needed every scrap of energy she had. And because she'd known she'd never survive losing anything she wanted as badly as love again.

Nathan had Neal again. Mandy had her grandfather and her new start in Rivermist. And Traci had her baby and the confidence to make her way, even if her parents didn't wise up and decide they needed to be part of it all.

What about me? Jenn asked herself.

What did she want? And did she have to guts to actually let herself reach for it, believing she could survive if it all went to hell again?

God, please don't let it be too late.

TRACI PULLED INTO the same gas station parking lot she'd first called Jenn from. She was crying so hard, she couldn't see to drive.

The last time she'd been there Jenn had promised that they'd make this work. That it was going to be okay somehow and that Traci wasn't alone. And she hadn't been, not for a second since she'd turned to the woman for help. Even when she'd packed her bags with every intention of heading for the bus station.

First Jenn and her father, and then Mr. Cain. She'd had adults around her every step of the way, making sure she was okay. Even having Mandy around had been great—as Traci had watched a living, breathing reason why going through with the abortion she'd wanted was never going to happen.

So how did she end up back here at this crummy gas station, feeling so totally alone?

Jenn was trying to make things sound so optimistic still, but even she had looked defeated back at the house. And if Jenn Gardner couldn't find a reason to keep believing, what the hell was the point?

Her friends were gone. Her parents would never accept her child. Even the one boy who'd loved her must have been relieved to get their "talk" out of the way yesterday, so he could get on with avoiding her like everyone else.

It was just her and her baby, and nothing Jenn said was going to make that sound any less lonely. She had years of getting used to lonely ahead of her, whether she was ready for it or not. Her dad didn't even think she could make it through junior college now, and maybe he was right. How the hell was she going to make college work on her own? Forget the school counselor's pep talk that she could do it. She couldn't look to the so-called friends or the guys who'd once swarmed around her for help—not the father of her baby, that's for sure. And she couldn't count on her parents, unless she went back to pretending to be exactly what they wanted her to be.

All she had was Jenn, who had a daughter of her own to worry about.

Traci had nothing.

Panic welled up along with the tears. Her dad was right! What kind of mother had a baby when she had nothing? Jenn had done it, but Traci wasn't that strong. She hadn't even been strong enough to stay and finish things with her parents. To see through a loser guy who refused to protect her with condoms and then had slapped her in the face instead of taking care of the new life he'd helped create.

Wiping at the trail of wetness running down her cheek, she pulled away from the gas station. Approaching one of the two stoplights in town, she slowed as the noise in her head increased, chanting *loser* and *I told you so* until she wanted to scream.

Night was closing in around her, and so was the future she'd been so sure she was ready for just a few months ago. Sure enough to ignore everything her parents had tried to teach her, throwing away her chance at the carefree tomorrow she'd never dreamed she could lose.

Mesmerized, she watched the stoplight ahead change to yellow, then to red.

Caution.

Stop.

Such obvious warnings.

Except what did warnings matter now, really, when she'd already ignored the most important ones…?

CHAPTER EIGHTEEN

"DAD!" JENN RACED UP to her father in the hospital waiting room, Neal's footsteps behind her announcing that he was still there. Thank God he'd been back from his run when her dad called. Jenn wasn't sure she'd have been able to drive herself. "What happened? Is Traci all right?"

Bob and Betty Carpenter were huddled in the corner, distraught and terrified. Despite their public battle with her father, he'd been the first person they'd called.

"She ran the red light at North and Chestnut," her father explained. "She hit another car at full speed."

"Oh, my God. How—"

"We don't know," her dad said. "I got here the same time as the Carpenters, just after the ambulance arrived. The ER staff were already working on Traci, and no one could tell us anything else. Someone from the sheriff's department is supposed to be on the way over."

"How could you let her drive when she was so

upset?" Bob Carpenter demanded from where he was holding a sobbing Betty to his chest. "The EMT said she must have been speeding through the intersection, given the amount of damage done to the cars. Do you understand? She was so upset, she ran the light on purpose!"

"No." Jenn's blood froze in her veins. Neal's arm came around her shoulder, encouraging her to lean against him. "Traci didn't run that light. I know her. I know how hard her decision was to keep this baby. To face what she'd done and make the most of it. There's no way she'd harm herself like this."

"Then explain it to me." The man pushed to his feet. "Explain to me how such a violent accident could have happened on one of our safest streets! Both cars were totaled. You convinced my daughter everything was going to be okay." He pointed a shaking finger at Jenn. "You let her believe that this would all magically work out. And when it didn't, she…she—"

"Bob." Jenn's father laid a hand on the man's shoulder. "Let's hear what the sheriff's department has to say before jumping to conclusions."

"What other conclusion is there?" Mr. Carpenter grabbed her father by the shoulders. "My daughter might be dying…. She's tried to hurt herself…. Because I made her feel like she couldn't come home. I made her…I made her think I didn't want her anymore…."

The sight of Traci's father weeping, the ugliness of what he was saying, memories of another father's grief in this same waiting room, ripped the floor out from under Jenn. Neal caught her against him, turned her to face him and held on, never saying a word.

He didn't have to. All he had to do was be there for her, and he was everything.

Everything she'd been afraid to believe in again.

Traci couldn't have…. She just couldn't have….

"Bob?" Sheriff Hamilton said from the doorway of the waiting area. Brett was standing just behind his father, worry and shock clouding his handsome young face. "Do you and Betty want to do this now, or do you want to wait until after you hear about Traci?"

"What happened?" Betty rushed across the room. "Can you tell us anything about why Traci would have done something like this? Could something have been wrong with the car?"

"What?" Sheriff Hamilton steadied her with a touch to her elbow. "No. Best we can tell, the car Traci was driving was running fine. She tried to brake. There were skid marks. But there was no way to stop at the speed she was spinning into the intersection."

"Spinning?" Bob joined his wife. "We were told she'd run the light."

"Yes, because of the other car that—"

"What other car?"

"The one that caused the accident." The sheriff shoved his hat back from his forehead. "What exactly did the EMTs tell you?"

"Nothing," Jenn's dad replied. "We made it here after they left."

"Then I think you folks need to sit down." The sheriff glanced toward Jenn, including her in his warning.

The Carpenters returned to the waiting room couch. Jenn couldn't sit. Sitting meant moving away from Neal, and she couldn't do that. Not now. The sheriff took his hat off to twirl it between his fingers.

"There was a third vehicle involved," he said. "Besides the one your daughter was driving in and the one her car hit. We have an eyewitness that saw Traci slowing as she approached the intersection, then another driver pulled into the passing lane and appeared to be trying to run her off the road. Traci must have accelerated or swerved, or both. She lost control of the car and spun through the intersection."

"Oh, dear God." Betty grasped for her husband's hand. "Who would try to run my daughter off the road?"

The sheriff glanced Jenn's way a second time, hesitating before answering.

The sick feeling that had been building in Jenn's stomach made a startling lurch upward.

"Your daughter was driving Ms. Gardner's car," the sheriff explained. "We think Jenn might have been the intended target."

"Someone was coming after me?" Jenn asked, horrified by what the sheriff's explanation could mean. "Oh, my God—Jeremy?"

"Yes, ma'am," Sheriff Hamilton confirmed. "Jeremy Compton just blew point-eight on his Breathalyzer test. He's been drinking all day, according to the bartender over at Bandit's. And for some reason he got it into his head to try and stop your car while Miss Carpenter was driving. When I left the scene he was babbling something about his kid and you living with Neal."

Everyone in the room was staring at Jenn, waiting for an answer. Everyone but Neal, who stood strong behind her, his support the only thing keeping her from collapsing on the floor.

"Are you telling me that my daughter's in there," Mr. Carpenter said, staring at Jenn, "because of you?"

"I…" She had no idea what to say, no idea how to process what was happening.

Jeremy… He wouldn't—

"Answer me!" Traci's father raged, shock giving way to anger.

"Bob." Jenn's father sat beside him. "I'm sure—"

"I've heard the rumors that boy's been spreading all over town," the other man said. "About Jenn and Neal, and how she slept with Jeremy years ago. If this was some kind of lovers triangle and—"

"Damn, Bob. You got this all figured out, don't you?" Nathan Cain of all people stepped into the room, Mandy at his side.

"What are you doing here, Dad?" Neal asked.

"I still have one car that's drivable," he said. And Jenn could have sworn his eyes twinkled as he glanced at his son. "I wanted to see how the Carpenter girl was doing."

The girl he'd been nothing but crotchety with from the moment she'd stepped foot inside his house.

"Nathan." Jenn's father crossed the room, his hand extended.

The warm shake that followed stunned everyone but Jenn. Her dad had found a way to visit Nathan last week, making her love him even more because of his concern for his old friend, rather than for whatever they'd argued about or what the community would think if he was seen at the Cain house. Now the two men were coming together out of concern for another man's child.

"It's good to see you again, Joshua." Nathan turned to the Carpenters, his demeanor that of the distinguished lawyer from years ago, instead of the grumbling hermit who'd been as vulgar as it took to run the entire town away. "Bob, Betty. I'm sorry to hear about Traci's accident. But—"

"I…I appreciate that, Nathan." Bob Carpenter took Nathan's outstretched hand and shook. "But we're—"

"If you think Jenn Gardner had anything to do with what's happened to Traci, you're full of crap."

"Excuse me?" Bob flushed. "Where do you get off—"

"I've spent more time with the woman in the last few weeks, and your child for that matter, than you have. So take my word for it. Jennifer Gardner's not to blame for a single wrong thing that's happened. Bad things just happen, Bob. Seems to me blaming anyone for it only causes more bad to follow."

You could have heard a pin drop. No one in the room could recall the last time they'd seen Nathan in public, let alone heard him wax philosophical about "live and let live."

The man winced, and some of the punch went out of his posture. With a sigh, he headed for the closest chair and sat.

"Are you okay?" Joshua asked when Jenn couldn't find her voice.

Nathan's complexion had grayed since he walked in the door. His hands were shaking now.

"Never been better," he said, regardless, nodding his head in Jenn's direction, "thanks to that girl over there. You two gentlemen, take care of your daughters." He took Mandy's hand as she came to stand beside him. "'Cause look what they go and make for you if you're lucky."

The longing in his words caught at Jenn's heart. So did the expressions on Bob and Betty Carpenter's faces as they finally let themselves see in Mandy what their own grandchild might look like.

"I'm going to take this little one to get some ice cream while we wait." Nathan made it to his feet again. "Seems to me I remember the cafeteria in this place having some pretty good ice cream."

Neal squeezed Jenn's shoulder as they watched his father go. When Nathan stumbled around the corner, Mandy helped steady him, then charged forward like the trouper she was.

Just helping a friend.

It's my turn.

Jenn looked up to see Neal's eyes glittering with unshed tears.

"Mr. and Mrs. Carpenter?" asked the doctor who stepped into the waiting area. He nodded at Jenn's dad and the sheriff as he walked over to Bob and Betty, then consulted the clipboard in his hand. "We were very lucky. The surgeon who consulted found no sign of internal injury, though we'll want to keep her under observation for at least twenty-four hours to be sure. She suffered a concussion and two broken ribs, but her seatbelt kept her away from the steering wheel." He dropped his clipboard to his side then, apology written all over his face, even though he'd just told them their daughter was going to be fine.

Jenn's head was slowly shaking. Her heart shattering for Traci. She knew what was coming, and she couldn't be there to hear it. She just couldn't.

"Your daughter mentioned her pregnancy to the firemen that cut her from the car," the doctor was saying as Jenn ran, leaving Neal's strength and warmth behind. "I'm sorry to have to tell you this, but…"

NEAL FOUND JENN SITTING ON an empty bed in a corner ER alcove, silently crying her eyes out.

Alone.

"You've got to stop this," he said. "You're not doing Traci any good hiding in here."

Her shoulders stiffened.

"Any good?" She jerked away when he wiped at the tears on her cheek. "Jeremy came after me, and now Traci's lost her baby."

"And she's going to need you there when the doctors tell her. You've been with her every step of the way during this pregnancy, and—"

"And now it's over, because of me!"

"You know better than that. You're a trained social worker. Do you take on the guilt of every young mother you know who loses a child?"

"No." She sprung off the bed, looking ready to hit

something, hit him for understanding. "I usually save it for the ones who miscarry because some creep from my past gets them mixed up with me!"

"Damn, Jenn. If Bob Carpenter knew you were this good at blaming yourself for everything, he wouldn't waste nearly as much time pointing his finger at you."

"Neal, stop—"

"No, I've been stopping. I've been jogging two and three times a day, leaving the room when you come in, trying to stay out of your way because that's what you needed. Now you stop!" He was done watching her slip away and pretending he was okay with it. And he was done watching her lose herself in other people's lives, when what she needed—what *he* needed—was for her to start living her own. "No one's blaming you for Traci's accident, except her terrified parents. A drunk took a swipe at the girl, and what's happened is horrible. But thinking it's your fault is just selfish."

"Selfish?"

"Yes, selfish." She might never forgive him for what he was about to say, but at least he'd know he'd tried. He was going to fight for her this time. Damn it, he was done running. The rest was up to her. "As long as you're mired in Traci's problems, you don't have to deal with feeling anything else, or take a chance on the life you're too afraid to want for yourself. You think I don't know that? That I don't know just how much wanting anything scares you to death?"

"You… I… I'm not using Traci…"

"You're hiding, same as I did, Jenn. You make your life about caring for everyone else, and I push people away while I help from a distance. But it's the same thing. We both end up alone in the end, exactly the way we want it." He needed to hold her, to make her listen. But this had to be her choice, or it would never work. "I used my dad's anger and then my work to push everything about this place away, and I waited too long to make myself come back. I've lost the last years of my dad's life, years I can't go back and relive because I'm so damn sorry I could puke. And now I'm pretty sure I've lost my chance with you, too, and…."

"Neal…" She reached for him, fresh tears falling.

He pulled her against his chest, cherishing her instinct to comfort him even though he knew it terrified her.

"And that's all right," he assured them both. "That would be okay, if we couldn't be together because we couldn't handle what happened to Bobby, or the years we've been apart. If it really was too late to try and start again. But every time I hold you I can feel how much you still love me. How much you still need what we had, just like I do. But then you pull away, because you're too afraid."

"I'm not afraid of you, Neal." She looked up at him. "I've never been afraid of you."

"Not of me." There was such passion in her insistence, in her heart, he didn't know how he'd ever let her go. "Of what being with me would mean. What letting someone into your heart again could cost you if everything went to hell. You've been hurt so badly, Jenn. And I was part of that. It's killing me to know you might never be able to trust your heart again."

"I…" She swallowed twice, as if to keep herself from continuing. Then those brave shoulders straightened, and she stepped back. "I love you, Neal. I'll always love you. But loving you makes me… You're right. The thought of losing you again terrifies me. And I…"

The fact that she couldn't finish saying it all didn't change the truth written all over her face.

She needed to be alone and safe more than she needed his love.

"I understand." He kissed her forehead, wishing to hell he didn't. If he hadn't spent so long running himself, maybe he could be angry at her for giving up. But all he could do now was understand, and somehow help make what she needed okay. "Don't worry, it's okay. You've given me my father back, Jennifer. You've let me be your friend again. Even let me help you just a little. It's more than I ever thought we'd have. For the rest of my life, I'll be grateful that I came back to Rivermist and found you here."

He brushed damp hair away from her face, kissed her one last time and turned away.

He had to get out of there.

"Neal, don't go," she begged.

"I'll meet you back at the house." He needed some time. He had to be anywhere but next to her while she told him she didn't have enough hope left to fight for the new beginning they'd almost had. "I...I think I'll go for a run."

"ARE YOU OKAY?" BRETT ASKED from where he sat on the edge of Traci's bed.

Jenn hesitated just outside the girl's room, still shaking from saying she loved Neal, then watching him walk away.

When the bruised teenager nodded from her nest of pillows instead of answering, Brett took her hand.

"Are you sure you don't want your parents?" he asked.

Traci shook her head, wincing and bringing a hand up to cup the bruise swelling from her right temple to her jawline.

"I can't face them," she finally said. "I know they're glad I lost the baby, and I just can't—"

"They're glad you're okay." Jenn stepped into the room. She couldn't let this child believe something like that. She couldn't watch love die here, too. "And they know you're hurting about the baby. They love you, Traci, don't turn them away now. Don't let yourself think you don't need them, just when you need love the most."

"She's right," Brett agreed. "I was there. Your mom started crying when she heard. I know you guys are still fighting, but they thought they'd lost you, and they're really upset about the baby. Let them come back here. They want to be with you."

Traci looked at Jenn, as the teen had done so many other times over the last few weeks, her eyes asking Jenn to tell her what to do. And Jenn's answer had to be the same as it had been from day one.

"You're the only one who knows what's right for you, sweetie. You have to follow your heart." *It's killing me to know you might never be able to trust your heart again.* "What... What does your heart tell you to do?"

Brett squeezed Traci's hand.

"I... I want my mom," Traci whispered on a sob.

Jenn ran, relieved that Traci was giving her future this final chance to work. Terrified that she herself had just let panic and fear keep her from grabbing onto what she'd dreamed of always having. She returned in less than a minute with Bob and Betty at her heels.

"Oh, honey." Betty engulfed her battered daughter in the gentlest hug Jenn had ever seen. "Thank God you're okay. We're so sorry about the baby, honey. So very sorry."

Traci looked at her father. "Really?"

When Bob stepped around the foot of the bed, Brett moved so the man could reach his daughter.

He gave Traci's bruised cheek a soft kiss.

"The baby meant the world to you, Traci, and you mean the world to me. I'm so sorry that you're hurting. I never wanted anything like this to happen to the ba… To my grandchild. I'm…" He wiped at the tear that had run from the corner of his eye to his jaw. "I'm so sorry, honey."

Seeing her father in tears got the best of Traci. She started sobbing, and then she was enveloped in her parents' hugs. In their love.

"Come home, Traci," Betty begged as she drew away. "Please, honey."

"If you want to," Bob added as he took his wife's hand, effectively forming a half circle around the teenager. "We want you home, honey, as much as we always have. But we heard you at dinner tonight. We almost lost you in that accident. It feels like we've been losing you for months. Because I've been too stubborn to let you grow up. You stay at the Cain house as long as you need. When you're ready to come home, we'll be there."

Traci looked at Bob Carpenter like he was once again the daddy she'd loved as a little girl, then her gaze moved to Jenn.

"You were right all along," she said, holding tight to her mother's hand, still bruised and crying, but healing where it was most important. "My heart *did* know exactly what to do."

CHAPTER NINETEEN

"I THOUGHT YOU were going for a run." Jenn found Neal sitting behind the wheel of the busted-up Mustang in his father's garage.

"I didn't really want to be anyplace but here." He smiled down at his lap instead of looking at her.

"Yeah." She approached slowly, watching him through the gaping hole where the windshield should have been. "I... Sometimes it takes something like Traci's accident to help you figure out what's really important. Where you really want to be."

"Or maybe it just takes time." His smile slipped away. "Timing is everything."

She wrenched open the banged-up passenger door and sat next to him in the car he and his father had gotten the chance to destroy, if not build, together.

"What are you reading?" She finally saw the papers strewn all over the inside of the car.

"Letters." He picked up a sealed envelope and ripped it open. An envelope that looked strangely familiar in the glare of the garage's bare lightbulb.

She reached for the papers closest to her, and Neal tensed. But he didn't stop her. The handwriting was instantly familiar, as was the jagged emotion written into every word.

"Oh, my God." She picked up another one, scanned the date, but couldn't bring herself to read a single word. "You... You said you never read these."

"I didn't." He ripped into another faded pink envelope. "Not before now. But I never could let them go. I couldn't keep myself from staring at them night after night in my cell. They were a part of you, the only part I thought I'd ever be able to touch again. Some days, having them was the only thing that got me through."

Tears flooded her eyes at the thought that she'd meant so much to him during a time when she'd been so sure he'd forgotten all about her.

Then what he was doing, what he was saying, took on another meaning entirely.

"Why... Why are you reading them now, out here in this trash heap of a car?"

Why wouldn't he look at her?

"I brought them back with me from Atlanta. I wanted you to have them. I wanted you to know... I didn't want you to think I hadn't needed you. That I didn't love you, even when I couldn't face you or anything else about this place." He finished reading the letter he held and passed it over. "But then everything that made you remember, everything about me, seemed to hurt you so much. I've kept them in my room. I was going to take them back with me to Atlanta when…" He ripped open another envelope. "I guess I finally needed to read them tonight. Because…"

Timing was everything.

"Because you've decided to leave?" She stacked the papers she held and passed them back, refusing to believe he was saying goodbye. "Here, take them back!"

"I'm not leaving now," he explained, tossing the paper and envelopes into a box at his feet. "It's just that after… When I'm not needed here anymore, I'm going back to my work in Atlanta. And I wanted you to know—"

"I know." She reached out and turned his face fully toward her. For the rest of her life, she'd never forget the shock of seeing the tears tracking down his cheeks. *God, please don't let it be too late.* "I know how much you love me, Neal."

She took the box and laid it on the dashboard.

My heart did *know exactly what to do,* Traci had whispered just a half hour earlier. The teenager's heart had led her back to her parents' love.

And Jenn had come looking for Neal.

"You know what you said at the hospital?" When

he didn't respond, her heart sank, but she wasn't giving up. Not this time. "About me being too afraid of this thing between us to give it another chance? Because I couldn't risk my heart and have it broken all over again?"

"Yeah," he finally said. He reached out and pulled her against him, kissing her hair. "And I understand, Jenn. More than I want to. It's not your fault. It's just the way things are."

He understood so well, he'd been sitting out here alone trying to find a way to say goodbye.

"Well, thanks to Traci Carpenter, I realized something else after you left. Something I learned for the first time when I watched you walk out of that courtroom when we were kids, and had been so sure I'd die from losing you."

"What?" he asked, memories from the worst day of both of their lives simmering in his voice.

"I remembered that I didn't die, Neal. I didn't give up, no matter how hard I tried. I guess I'm like you. I'm just not made that way. No matter how bad things got, or how hopeless life seemed, I kept going, the same way Traci has. The same way you did. Somehow along the way I got being alone mixed up with being safe. I was so busy making a life for my daughter, and hiding in other people's problems, that I let myself believe it was better not to trust the heart I thought had died when I lost you. But I survived, and I made it back here somehow. Just like you. It's a miracle, really, when you think about it. The way caring about our fathers got us to do what we've spent the last eight years running from."

"What are you saying, Jennifer?" His strong hands cupped her face.

She loved the way he said her name. The way the hope shining in his eyes wrapped around her heart.

She loved him.

"I'm saying I never really wanted to be alone, Neal. My heart never really died. It's been right here, all along. Waiting for you. No matter how scary it may be, or what happens next, you're what my heart wants, what it's always wanted. I love you. I always have. And I don't know how to give up on that."

She kissed him first this time, and she kept on kissing him. Reminding herself with each touch, each gentle word that he murmured as he kissed her back, exactly why she was willing to risk anything, to hold on to the perfect piece of now that she held in her arms.

EPILOGUE

"GRANDPA, THEY'RE ABOUT to start the dancing!" Mandy squealed. And despite the sound of her daughter's laughter, Jenn felt her eyes fill with tears.

They were missing one very special grandpa today.

She glanced up from where she sat at Nathan Cain's kitchen table to see her father pull Mandy close, a suspicious sheen of moisture coating his eyes as well. They were having a party. The entire town had turned out. Buford was in the corner chatting with Dr. Harden. Traci and Brett and a bunch of the kids were on the porch outside. The once-empty house was packed. And everyone had vowed there would only be laughter today—to celebrate the life of the man who'd become special to them again, even if it had only been for a short time.

Nathan's wake was the social event of the season, bringing together the community that had rallied around him the last month of his life, no matter how much he'd griped and complained about the attention. After Jenn and Traci had mentioned his ill health at the church council meeting, and after his appearance at the hospital to make sure Traci was okay, it was no wonder that Southern hearts had started to melt up and down North Street. Long made-up minds had started to change. Traci had also let it slip to her parents how he'd confronted Jeremy Compton that awful night the creep had come to the house. How a sick and limping Nathan had stood between the town princess and a boy no one had known at the time could be so dangerous. And that was that. Nathan had become an honest-to-goodness local hero.

Bob and Betty Carpenter had been the first family to bring a home-cooked meal over to share, their way of thanking Nathan for all he'd done for their daughter. But they had been in no way the last neighbors to offer whatever help they could. Even Brett and his friends had arrived one afternoon, and returned like clockwork for weeks, adding their muscle to the endless home improvement that remained to be done on the house. Until just a week ago, when the work had finally been finished.

Nathan slipped into a coma in his sleep the very next day, and he'd drifted away the following night. But he'd seen his home restored to its former beauty. He'd seen that the town he'd once loved hadn't forgotten him after all. And he and Neal had finally had their talk.

A real one this time, in which nothing was dented or destroyed, and very few words had actually been spoken. But around midnight one night, when the wind had settled down enough for the two of them to sit on the porch and watch the stars the way they once had with Neal's mom, Neal had told his father he loved him. Then he'd cried in Jenn's arms when he'd come upstairs to bed. Because in a gruff, almost impossible-to-hear voice, his father had said he loved Neal, too.

The doorbell rang.

Jenn watched as her fiancé crossed the foyer to answer it, the suit coat he'd worn to the funeral discarded and his tie askew. Nathan wasn't the only one the town had decided to accept after the events surrounding Traci's accident.

Neal opened the door to none other than Catherine Compton. Her about-face change in opinion toward the Cain family had been the most dramatic of all. It couldn't have been easy for her to face first Traci's parents and then Jenn's father, after what Jeremy had done. Coming to visit Nathan, after the things she'd said about him and Neal, had to have been the hardest gesture of all. But she'd made the effort, and she'd shaken Neal's hand as she left that day, beginning to see in him what so many others already had. Redemption instead of past mistakes. A man who could be a trusted friend, if he were only given another chance. And maybe in forgiving him, Catherine had finally begun to put Bobby's death behind her.

Neal showed Catherine in, then he looked Jenn's way, his troubled gaze softening into the smile that warmed her heart every time she saw it. Jeremy was being held without bond, pending his DUI and vehicular battery charges. A simple comparison of blood types had been all they'd needed to rule him out as Mandy's father. His bitterness and anger couldn't hurt Jenn or anyone else now, but his threats and accusations and mixed-up anger had cost an unborn life, when the person he'd really been gunning for was Jenn. Seeing him or Catherine wasn't going to be pleasant for Jenn for quite a while to come.

In the den, classic jazz began playing from the stereo system. The music Nathan had made Jenn and Neal listen to as kids for hours on end, then had played night after night over the last month as they had learned to trust in their love for each other all over again. Neal came toward her, his hand reaching out as their friends and neighbors looked on. He led her into the den, where they'd removed all the furniture just for today, and pulled her close. They began to slow dance to Nathan's favorite Miles Davis album, holding tight to each other as the memories wrapped them in slow, smooth notes from the past.

There could be no more perfect moment, no more perfect feeling, than laying her head on the shoulder of the man she loved, and believing with all her heart that he would still be there holding her tomorrow. Loving her. Marrying her in just a few months. They'd be saying their vows in this very room in fact, with her father officiating and Mandy giving Jenn away.

And though there were tears in her heart for Nathan, there was also the laughter he'd wanted for this day. So as she looked up, smiled at Neal and noticed her father dancing with Mandy nearby, she gave herself over to the beauty of the music Nathan had loved. The perfection of the future he'd played such a cantankerous role in bringing about for all of them.

Stability is highly overrated….

Dana Logan's world had always revolved around her children. Now they're all grown up and don't seem to need anything she's able to give them. Struggling to find her new identity, Dana realizes that it's about time for her to get "off her rocker" and begin a new life!

Off Her Rocker

by Jennifer Archer

Available August 2006
TheNextNovel.com

HARLEQUIN®
Next™

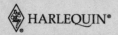

HARLEQUIN®

American ROMANCE®

American Beauties

SORORITY SISTERS,
FRIENDS FOR LIFE

Michele Dunaway

THE MARRIAGE CAMPAIGN

Campaign fund-raiser Lisa Meyer has worked
hard to be her own boss and will let nothing—
especially romance—interfere with her success.
To Mark Smith, Lisa is the perfect candidate for
him to spend his life with. But if she lets herself
fall for Mark, will she lose all she's worked for?
Or will she have a future that's more than
she's ever dreamed of?

On sale August 2006

Also watch for:

THE WEDDING SECRET
On sale December 2006

NINE MONTHS NOTICE
On sale April 2007

Available wherever Harlequin books are sold.

HARLEQUIN® *Romance*

A family saga begins to unravel
when the doors to the Bella Lucia
Restaurant Empire are opened...

The Brides of Bella Lucia

*A family torn apart by secrets,
reunited by marriage*

AUGUST 2006

Meet Rachel Valentine, in
HAVING THE FRENCHMAN'S BABY
by Rebecca Winters

Find out what happens when a night of passion is followed
by a shocking revelation and an unexpected pregnancy!

SEPTEMBER 2006

The Valentine family saga continues with
THE REBEL PRINCE by Raye Morgan

BRINGS YOU THE LATEST IN

Vicki Hinze's

WAR GAMES

MINISERIES

Double Dare

December 2005

A plot to release the deadly DR-27
supervirus at a crowded mall? Not U.S.
Air Force captain Maggie Holt's idea of
Christmas cheer. Forget the mistletoe—
Maggie, with the help of scientist
Justin Crowe, has to stop a psycho
terrorist before she can even think of
enjoying Christmas kisses.

Available at your favorite retail outlet.